I0772866

VALERIE MASSEY GOREE

Dangerous Dalliance

Sisters in Peril, Book 1

Valerie Massey Goree

BookViral review of *Windrush*
"A delightful dalliance into pure escapism..."

"***Forever Under Blue Skies*** made me want to visit Australia. The two mysteries woven into the story kept me turning the pages and the proposal was so romantic, I had to read it twice."

*Amazon Reader Review

CHAPTER 1

Determined to handle the anniversary of her fiancé's disappearance like any other day, Jan Sullivan hauled her backpack to a wooden bench in Canfield Park. She had one goal—to complete the commissioned sketches for a children's book. With the pad on her lap and her favorite Faber-Castell graphite pencil in hand, she studied the raucous activity of children on the playground equipment. Situated in a family neighborhood on the north side of San Antonio, the park was a favorite of the many kids in the area. They provided ideal models and were out in full force enjoying the cool but pleasant afternoon weather.

Jan had already captured images of children on the jungle gym, climbing the mini rock wall, or swishing down slides, and the hero and heroine of the story hunting for clues behind bushes or in the sandbox. She'd planned the sketches to match the script for each page, and today, youngsters on the swings were her target.

A nearby toddler's giggle brought a smile to Jan's face. She hadn't felt that content for a long time and puffed out a sigh. Months ago, she'd realized January, 11 was just a date on the calendar. If Bryan suddenly returned to her life, she'd be relieved but wouldn't marry him. Over time, she'd identified one of the main reasons—his materialism. He was overly concerned about how much money he earned. Spent a lot of time deciding which outlandishly expensive vehicle to purchase next. And, the main reason, she realized she didn't love him enough to spend the rest of her life with him. Maybe that's why he left. He sensed she couldn't surrender herself to his often self-centered demands. Why then did she feel responsible for his disappearance?

As she set pencil to parchment, her phone chirped. Sliding it out of her jacket pocket, she noted no name appeared with the number. Nothing unusual about that. She often received unsolicited business calls.

"Jan Sullivan speaking."

"Afternoon, Ms. Sullivan." The gruffness of the man's voice sounded muffled. "Where is Bryan Buchanan?"

Surely she hadn't heard correctly. "Excuse me?"

"Don't be coy. Where's Bryan?"

A gust of wintry air forced icy tentacles through her jacket to stab her heart. Bryan Buchanan, her…fiancé.

Despite her earlier *joie de vivre*, painful memories

of his unexplained abandonment resurfaced. She clutched the sketchpad to her chest. "I don't know."

"It's January, 11. Aren't you thinking about him today?"

The caller knew when Bryan disappeared.

Contentment oozed away as her heart rate accelerated. Blood tha-thumped in her head. "Who are you? Why do you need to know where he is?"

"Doesn't matter who I am." His words dripped with anger. "I won't leave you alone until I get what I want." He paused for a couple of seconds. "I know where you live."

A dull ping severed the call. Jan stared at the phone while a shudder wormed its way across her shoulders. The man wanted something besides Bryan's whereabouts. Rattled but still in control, she scrolled to *calls received* and hit *send* on the most recent. It rang and rang but no one answered.

She shoved her phone back into her pocket and glared at her blank sketchpad. So much for her plan. Even though perfect subjects surrounded her, the mysterious phone call numbed her fingers and gave life to a seed of fear. Why did the caller think she knew anything about Bryan's disappearance? Recalling the underlying threat in his words, the thumping in her head increased. Her efforts to keep her past from intruding on her present had failed.

A troop of little girls climbed onto the swings in front of her. Their squeals of joy reminded Jan of her reason for being at the park. Inhaling cool air, she resolved she wouldn't allow a phone call to dictate her actions. She squared her shoulders and set to work.

Focused on the laughing kids, she produced pages of detailed sketches. With each pencil swirl, the heavy mood lifted as light crept into the dark corners of her soul. Bryan and the conjured-up man asking about him became faint silhouettes.

After studying one picture, Jan added more detail to the girl's flying tresses and tilted her head. She allowed a small smile of satisfaction to touch her lips and nodded once. "That's it."

In a fluid motion, she turned to a clean page and outlined another child.

"Sophie! Watch where you're going!"

Jan raised her head at the masculine yell.

Heedless of the warning, a little three- or four-year-old girl raced toward the swings on a path to an inevitable collision.

Tossing aside her sketchpad, Jan lurched forward and snatched up the child. "Whew, that was close." She set the girl down on the grass and placed her hands on the tot's tiny shoulders. "Are you okay?"

Huge blue eyes dominated the scared little face.

Before the child could answer, a man rushed over and reworded the question. "Sophie, are you all right?" He fell to his knees in front of her.

"Daddy, why are you yelling? Why did she grab me?" The child's wide-eyed stare flew from her father's face to Jan.

"Honey, this lady saved you from getting hit. You weren't looking where you were going." Sophie wrapped her arms around his neck as he picked her up and stood. Smiling, he turned to Jan. "Thank you."

"Glad I got to her in time."

"I'm grateful for your quick action." He kissed his daughter's cheek and extended his hand toward Jan.

Its warmth surprised her. She raised her gaze to his face and took in his dark brown wavy hair and blue eyes, the color of his daughter's, before he withdrew his hand.

"Thanks again." He inclined his head and carried Sophie to the opposite side of the playground.

Jan returned to the bench to retrieve her sketchpad and pencil which had fallen onto the pea gravel. Dirt smudges covered the page she'd been working on. She tore it out, sat down, and stared at the clean sheet. Even with the deadline looming, the incident with the man and his daughter derailed her concentration.

After resting the pencil behind her ear, Jan squeezed her hands together. Warmth the man's hand had generated lingered. A little butterfly somersaulted in her stomach. His dark hair emphasized his blue eyes which reminded her of the Mediterranean Sea. It had been a long time since she'd noticed the color of a man's eyes. It had been a long time since she'd noticed a man. Period.

Removing the pencil, Jan nibbled its end. If she

was going to notice men again, maybe she shouldn't begin with a guy who was probably married. She shook her head, but her mental image of the dimple hovering at the corner of his mouth refused to budge. Despite the threatening phone call and the guilt she'd carried since Bryan's disappearance, a slit opened in her cold heart. *If blue eyes and a warm handshake could spark such interest, imagine what a whole man could do.*

While she studied the last sketch she'd done, Sophie and her father paraded past the bench, hand-in-hand.

He stopped, and Sophie slipped her hand free.

"Daddy, can I play in the sandbox?"

"Sure, but stay where I can see you."

Chestnut-brown braids bobbed as she skipped.

He waited until she settled in the box, then asked, "Mind if I join you?"

"Not at all." Jan dumped her backpack on the ground.

Seated at an angle allowed him to face Jan and keep an eye on his daughter. "Thank you again for stopping her. Sophie gets so excited sometimes. I have a hard time keeping up with her."

"I don't have any kids." *An odd nugget of information to share with a stranger.*

He glanced at her sketchpad. "You sure know how to draw them. Who's the little girl?"

As he pointed to the picture—a girl in full pump, hair flying, cares forgotten—Jan noticed no wedding ring.

"No one in particular. She embodies all kids who thrill at the swing's motion."

"I see that. Makes me want to jump on a swing." His warm laugh washed over her.

Imagine him flying through the air. Jan joined in the laughter.

Again he pointed to the pad in her lap. "Why are you sketching kids on swings?"

Was he merely being polite because she'd helped his daughter, or did he have a genuine interest? It didn't matter because she'd probably never see him again. "I illustrate children's books and I'm working on one titled *Flossie the Ferret's Playground Adventure.* The author wants old-fashioned paintings, not computer-generated pictures or cartoonish kids and animals. The sketches are due next week."

"No kidding. Have you sketched the ferret yet?"

Chuckling, Jan turned to the beginning of her pad. "Here's Flossie. I spent many hours in a pet shop with their pair of ferrets. They were so much fun."

"I can imagine. How do you know what to draw? I mean, do you make lots of sketches and then decide which ones to use?"

"Exactly. I have the prose from the story broken down page by page. My accompanying pictures must complement the words. So yes, I sketch way more than I need, then at home, I'll choose the most appropriate drawing, add the respective prose, and send them to the art director for approval."

"I read to Sophie every night but I've never considered how much effort is behind the words and pictures. What books have you illustrated?"

Jan named a few. "But my favorite is the *Mr. Caterpillar* series written by Pete Andrews."

"I've heard of him. In fact, my sister recommended I purchase his books for Sophie's birthday. I'll have to check out *Mr. Caterpillar*."

"There are five in the set. I consider them my best work so far."

"A book illustrator. I've never met one before."

"I also paint landscapes and portraits. I have space in *La Casa de Colores* gallery downtown." She added way more detail than she'd intended.

"That's interesting—" His phone beeped. He nabbed it from his pocket and viewed the screen. "Sorry, I have to take this." Stepping away a few feet, he conversed in a low tone.

Jan flipped the page and searched the playground for another subject.

When Sophie's father returned to the bench, a frown creased his brow. "Sophie and I need to leave." He withdrew a thin silver case from his back pocket and extracted a card. "Here's my business card. If ever you need my help, please give me a call." As Jan reached for the yellow and blue card, his fingers lingered on it. "Seriously." His gaze raked her face for a moment before he let go.

"Thank you." She scanned the print. *KC Hatcher, M.A.; M.Ed. Licensed Professional Counselor. Specializing in Christian-based Principles.*

He strode to the sandbox and took Sophie's hand. They crossed the playground and zigzagged through the parking lot.

Jan gave his card another peek and noted his office was close by. Did he think she needed his professional services or was his gesture merely a sincere *thank you*? As she slipped the card into her pocket she wondered if the anxiety brought on by the phone call showed on her face. If it did, her emotional state was none of his business.

Giving herself a mental shake, Jan settled her sketchpad firmly on her lap. But her pencil lay idle. For the most part, her life since Bryan's disappearance satisfied her. She enjoyed the company of her two sisters and friends from university and her rewarding career as an independent artist filled her time. She had ventured out on several dates, but none of the men sparked the slightest glimmer of interest. Yet, today, the simple act of keeping a stranger's child from danger emphasized the void in her life.

The what-if game came calling. What if she had a little girl who liked to run in the park? What if Bryan hadn't left and she married him? Her mood darkened along with the sky.

Children's laughter interrupted her daydream. She rubbed her cold hands together. If only she could warm her heart as easily. Focusing again on the swings in front of her where two young boys were trying to swing in rhythm, she straightened the pad on her lap. Pencil in hand she sketched their body movements, reveling in the scritching of lead on parchment.

Her concentration was interrupted by the faint words of a song drifting up behind her. At first, she ignored the intrusion, but she recognized a taunt when she heard one. She turned as the intensity of the lyrics increased. Two boys, probably eight or nine years old, followed a younger boy in a wheelchair, tossing gravel at him as he tried to maneuver his chair across the lawn. An icy knot squeezed Jan's stomach. The teasing jeer that plagued her kindergarten year bombarded her eardrums. She shook her head. No, she would not allow an ugly period in her childhood to keep her from intervening.

Jan stood ready to rescue the young boy, however, an older kid jogged over to him and pushed his chair to the sidewalk, yelling over his shoulder, "Get a life. If you have to pick on someone, choose a kid your own age who's not in a wheelchair."

Although Jan didn't completely agree with the statement, she smiled at them as they passed her. Kids could be so cruel. She sat and studied her last sketch and added an untied shoelace to one subject, and a backward baseball cap to the other.

A cold wind stirred the dead oak leaves under the bench. Fat drops of water splattered on her sketchpad.

Screaming children and yelling parents announced the rain's arrival. With a groan, Jan snatched up her backpack, rammed the pad inside, and raced to her car. Completing the sketches had to wait. Besides, she'd forgotten her lapboard. She should have known better than to sit on a hard bench hunched over her sketchpad for hours on end. The resulting twinges in her back elicited painful memories of her long-ago spinal fusion surgery.

The drive home wouldn't take long, but Jan dreaded spending the evening alone. She'd been fine until the phone call which gnawed at her gut. Before the threatening words, she'd believed Bryan left because he didn't want to marry her, but the caller hinted at a more sinister reason. Turning left at the light, she stopped at her favorite pizza parlor and after ordering, called her middle sister and invited her over.

"So sorry, sis. I can't join you tonight. I'm moving into the house where I'll be pet-sitting for three weeks. The owners leave early tomorrow." Delaney offered house-and-pet-sitting services to earn money and to provide nicer places to live than sharing a small apartment with Emily, her high school friend. "I'll call you tomorrow."

Disappointment covered Jan like a leaden shawl. She'd eat alone in her big house. With an ache growing in her heart, she paid for the pizza. Savory aromas of cheese, pepperoni, and peppers exuded from the box as it warmed her hands.

The rain had stopped. Streetlight glistened off the wet tarmac, and people huddled into their coats as they hurried along. Jan climbed into her SUV. She shivered as she drove through the neighborhood. More than the outside temperature chilled her to the core.

She gave up her feeble attempts to be nonchalant. Maybe it was the rain that finally got to her.

It had also rained the day Bryan left.

Loss engulfed her, sapping every ounce of life out of her body. She concentrated on her driving as she followed the familiar route home. Stopped at a traffic light, she glanced at the black sedan in the next lane. The driver, wearing a baseball cap low on his forehead, leered at her, but quickly turned to his companion. When the light changed, Jan thought nothing more about the incident as the other car zoomed ahead.

Thick, dark clouds brought on an early dusk. Jan turned down her street where an on-coming vehicle's high beams blinded her. Blinking, she hugged the right side of the road, but the car careened straight for her. Jan honked the horn and flashed her lights. The car kept coming, now yards away. Heat surged up from her boots, her breath came in short spurts. Her hands ached gripping the wheel. Parked cars lined the opposite side of the street. She couldn't escape. The lights were mere feet away. She braced for impact, but the car veered and skimmed by her. It screeched around the corner and disappeared.

Her driveway beckoned and Jan roared into it.

Pressing the remote with quivering fingers, she drove into her garage, quickly closed the door, and remained in the vehicle as if glued to the seat. The seed of fear sprouted roots that forced their way through Jan's body. Blood pounded like thundering ocean waves in her head.

A sliver of sanity admonished her. "You can't sit out here all night." She sucked in a breath, balanced the pizza box on her backpack, and scurried inside, setting the alarm system before dumping everything on the kitchen table. As she hung up her jacket, her cell phone rang. She glared at the screen.

Another number without a name. The same one? She couldn't remember.

In no emotional state to endure more harassment, she allowed the call to go to voicemail. Jan sank into a chair and waited for the message beep. Tapping the icon with a shaking index finger, she held her breath.

"Where'd you learn to drive like that?" Not the same voice as before. "Next time we meet, you'd better tell me what I want to know."

Her nails dug into her palms as she pounded her fists on the table. "What *do* you want?"

CHAPTER 2

On the way home, Hatch had stopped at Milly's Books 'N Things, a store close to his office. They did not have the whole set of *Mr. Caterpillar* books, so he'd placed an order and left with their lone copy of *Mr. Caterpillar Builds a House*. The ride home had been unusually quiet with Sophie examining the book in her car seat. He'd wait to check out Ms. Sullivan's artwork when he read the story to Sophie at bedtime.

Later, he served the casserole he'd prepared that morning with his mind anywhere but on the task.

"Daddy, are you angry with me?" Sophie's words jolted Hatch's attention back to the present.

"No, honey. Why do you think that?"

"'Cause you're not talking."

"Sorry, Sophie. I'm not mad at you. I was thinking about the lady we met at the park. The one who saved you from the swing."

"I...was scared when she picked me up. But I didn't get hurt."

"That's the main thing. And you'll be more careful

next time. Right?"

"Uh-huh."

He ruffled her hair and then tweaked her cheek.

"Quit, Daddy. Can I go now?"

"Sure. Take your plate to the kitchen, and you can play for about thirty minutes."

While he drained his glass of iced tea, he listened for her quick footsteps as they echoed down the hall to the den where her toys lay scattered about. She was so tiny, but she occupied such a huge space in his heart. Recalling the near collision in the park again, he thumped the table. What would he do if he lost Sophie? He blamed himself for his wife's death, and if Sophie had been hit, that would have been his fault, too.

But the woman with the haunting gray eyes had rescued her.

He carried his dishes to the sink and concentrated on cleaning up, but those eyes wouldn't leave him alone. Once he'd started the dishwasher, he made his way to the office where he collapsed into the leather chair.

Being self-employed meant he always had mounds of paperwork, billing, and filing. He ignored the cluttered desk as he rocked back and forth, lost in studying the photographs displayed next to his computer. Laura holding newborn Sophie. His sister and brother-in-law, and other family pictures—one taken three weeks before Laura's death. Familiar sadness and regret swamped him. A minute passed in silence. He wiped his hand across his face to dissolve the memories and turned to sort the papers on his desk.

As he worked, he couldn't stop his mind from drifting back to the park to the woman who'd helped Sophie. The brief encounter had captivated him. Obviously, she enjoyed her career, but those eyes—large, sad, and as cold as an arctic lake, plagued him. Something troubled her.

Billing and scheduling forgotten, his gaze drifted to the photos of Laura again. When he admired a woman or enjoyed a date he no longer felt disloyal. She would want him to be happy. Hatch tented his fingers. His bare ring finger reminded him he hadn't found another woman to share the rest of his life. Turning off the computer, he pushed back from the desk, left the office, and called for Sophie to put away her toys.

With her bath-time ritual complete, he carried her over his shoulder to her bedroom and before setting her down, took one last sniff of her shampooed baby-soft hair.

She skipped to the bookshelf. "Where's my new book?"

"Silly me. I left it in the living room. Jump into bed while I get it."

When he returned, she had her pink princess duvet tucked around her little body, and Patches Panda, her favorite stuffed animal rested on her pillow. He sat next to her and began reading. He took his time so they could devour the pictures and the words. Ms. Sullivan sure was talented.

Succumbing to Sophie's repeated requests, he read the story again.

After the second reading, she hugged the book. "I like *Mr. Caterpeeper*." Her oversized lavender pajamas smothered her little arms.

He chuckled at her mispronunciation. "Now it's time for prayers."

She climbed out of bed, knelt beside him, and offered innocent words of thanks.

Hatch listened and then added, "Father, thank You for the woman at the park who helped Sophie today. Bless her and ease her pain."

A familiar but disquieting emotion stirred in his chest. He couldn't stop thinking about those sad eyes.

CHAPTER 3

Savoring the pungent aroma of her coffee, Jan perused the sketches she'd done the previous day.

"I like that one and that one." She took a sip of coffee and flipped through more pages. "Not that one and definitely not that one. I'll have to go back to Canfield Park."

Moxie, a gray tabby, ignored her mistress's words and strutted out of the kitchen.

A brief flash of father and daughter brought a quick grin to Jan's face. She could produce the needed sketches at home but maybe she'd see the pair again.

Her phone rang. She stiffened as her smile faded. The anonymous man from last night? Before going to bed, she'd called the police to report the car that nearly rammed her, and that both harassing phone calls came from the same number—which she'd programmed into her contacts under the name *Crank*. The officer said they'd check her phone records to determine who made the calls, but without additional evidence, they could do nothing more.

Jan decided against calling her eldest sister, Teagan, a detective in the San Antonio Police Department's Financial Crimes Unit. As the other officer said, there wasn't much evidence to go on. Besides, Teagan was in the middle of an undercover assignment and probably wouldn't have answered her call.

Following the fifth ring, Jan picked up her phone can checked caller ID. Not Crank, but Marybeth Buchanan. Releasing her imprisoned breath, she melted into the chair. "Good morning." Her voice cracked.

"What's good about it? I'm still grieving, you know."

The familiar voice of her almost mother-in-law grated against her eardrums, but she replied in a rehearsed calm tone, "How can I help you, Marybeth?"

"I have questions. I'm coming over."

The woman ended the call before Jan could respond. She placed her empty cereal bowl in the sink and hurried to the front door. When Marybeth said she'd be right over, she'd be right over! She lived three doors down.

Marybeth had bought the house right after the engagement. Jan considered moving several times in the year since Bryan departed, but she loved her house and had spent considerable time and money converting a bedroom into an art studio.

Jan expected the knock but jumped anyway. She opened the door and attempted a welcoming smile.

"Would you like a cup of coffee?"

Barging straight in, Marybeth ignored the small formal living room and stomped down the hall to the kitchen. Her defiant stride brokered no argument. "Yes."

Jan closed the door and followed the woman. She placed a pod in the coffee machine and readied a mug. When it filled, she set it in front of Marybeth.

Without a word of thanks, Marybeth sat at the round kitchen table and scooped several spoons of sugar into her cup.

Jan picked up her mug but had no desire to share a convivial moment with this woman. She cleared her throat and sat down. "What's on your mind?"

Arms folded, Marybeth glared at Jan. "It's been a year, you know. What are you doing about it? You haven't proven to me that you didn't kill him."

Jan bristled. "I did not kill your son. Why can't you believe me when I tell you he's alive?"

Sipping coffee, Marybeth averted her eyes and frowned. "He was my baby." In the silence that followed, her gaze darted back and forth, and then her head jerked up. "Alive? How do you know he's alive?"

Jan drummed her fingernails on her ceramic mug. She'd already given Marybeth the information but obviously needed to repeat it. Anything to get the woman off her back. "Soon after he disappeared, his good friend from work, Eduardo Fernandez, told me Bryan had moved out of state. He gave me no further information. Then a few months later, I noticed Bryan's jacket in the hall closet, and the DVDs and CDs he loaned me were gone. You know how he loves his old movies and music."

"And how'd he get in? Break a window?" Marybeth's words dripped with sarcasm.

Nothing new in that. Jan ignored her tone. "He had a key so he could feed my cat when I went out of town, and I never thought to change the locks until he took his items."

The woman sneered over the rim of the coffee mug.

Jan decided to share another reason. "Remember the flowers I chose for my wedding bouquet?"

"Purple and white things."

"Calla lilies and ranunculus. Last year I received two bouquets that included those flowers. In April on our chosen wedding date, and later in June on my birthday."

"Phooey. Many people knew those dates." Marybeth's sneer remained.

"True. But only you, Bryan, and my sisters, knew which flowers I'd selected."

"Maybe you sent them to yourself."

Where did Marybeth get her ideas? Jan supposed if all those details didn't convince her, adding the recent phone call about him probably wouldn't either.

With a sniff, Marybeth wiped a tear from her wrinkled cheek.

Jan's ire thawed. Memories of light-hearted gatherings with Marybeth and Bryan, and shared stories of his childhood took its place.

But considering the woman's disjointed thoughts and odd behavior, Jan had to ask, "Are you taking your medication?" She attempted to touch Marybeth's gnarled hand but she snatched it away.

The grim line of her mouth didn't bode well for a peaceful conclusion to the meeting. Without warning, Marybeth stood with such force her chair crashed to the floor.

Jan jerked back from the table.

"Why is everyone asking about my pills? Of course, I'm taking them, but what business is it of yours?" She wiped spots of sweat off her forehead. "Quit trying to change the subject. Bryan was going to break off the engagement and you found out. That's why you killed him." Her eyes narrowed. "You know what he told me once? He said you were always going on and on about how you couldn't lift heavy items. You...you had something wrong with you back. Scolil...scolis—"

"Scoliosis."

"Right, and you had things in your spine to keep it straight."

What did her medical history have to do with Bryan's disappearance? "I do have rods in my back."

The surly expression on Marybeth's face blended in with her wrinkles. "He didn't believe you. He said you used that as an excuse to avoid rock climbing with him or to join him in his kickboxing sessions. And your back is as straight as mine."

"Now it is." Jan frowned. Bryan saw her scars every time she wore a bathing suit. Had he really doubted her scoliosis diagnosis as a child, or was Marybeth confused? Jan could have listed all the surgeries she had to adjust the expandable rods. Every six months from age five to twelve. She could sing the song that kids had made up about her, the song brought to mind so forcefully by the kids teasing the boy in the wheelchair.

Jan shook her head. The woman didn't seem to be in any frame of mind to comprehend details Jan provided. She inhaled and said as calmly as she could, "Please leave, Marybeth."

"Not before I tell you I know where you buried Bryan. Under that tree in your backyard." Leaning toward Jan, she scowled. "Go ahead. I dare you. Dig it up and prove me wrong."

Jaw gaping, Jan circled the table. "You think I buried Bryan in my backyard? Okay, Marybeth, that's enough. Go. Now."

The older woman stormed down the hall and out the door, shutting it with a resounding slam.

Jan sank into the nearest chair, her whole body quivering. No matter how absurd Marybeth's accusation was, it concerned her, as did the enraged tone in her own voice. *Get a grip.*

After righting Marybeth's chair, Jan rinsed out the mugs. She rescued her sketchpad from the floor where it had landed in the fracas and raced upstairs as if escaping the foul atmosphere Marybeth left in the room.

Sunlight streaming through the studio's large windows did little to heal the rift in her soul. Fingers clutching the pad, she stepped to the window facing the backyard. Resting her forehead on the cold glass, she stared at the Monterey Oak sapling Marybeth wanted to dig up.

"Bryan, where are you?" Like it or not, this morning's painful visit and the harassing phone calls forced him back into her life. But not her heart.

She stood a moment longer, then slumped against the wall and surveyed the studio. Several unfinished canvases were stacked on the floor. Completed landscapes occupied another corner. Paint tubes, brushes, and other materials covered the counter near the sink. She cleaned the oil paint off her brushes outside, but lingering whiffs of oils and turpentine hung in the air.

This world had been her salvation when Bryan had left. She'd spent weeks painting landscapes of the Texas Hill Country, which had garnered her a permanent showing in the gallery. Over the following months, she'd accepted Bryan's departure and attempted to carve out a new future.

The events in the park the previous day and

Marybeth's visit sent Jan's brain into overdrive. Yes, Bryan had disappeared three months before their wedding date, but the more she dwelt on their last few months together, the more she was convinced their relationship had unraveled long before he left. Marybeth's words today confirmed Bryan had similar feelings.

On the anniversary of his abandonment, her heart should have felt empty, but it didn't.

The brief encounter in the park had opened her eyes and heart to new possibilities. Even if she never saw Mr. Hatcher and Sophie again—although he was hard to forget—she knew she was well on her way to being free of Bryan. If only he'd contact her to say he was okay and explain why he left. Her old insecurities were never far from the surface. Was he simply another boyfriend who broke off their relationship because she wasn't worth his time? Sure, he was the only one who'd proposed, but—

Her cell phone rang. She jumped at the intrusion and pried it out of her blue jeans pocket. Delaney. Sliding down the wall, she plopped onto the floor.

"Hey." Her voice wobbled with relief.

"Hi, sis. Sorry, I couldn't have supper with you last night. I've settled in for my new job taking care of two dogs and a cat, and my second term begins next week. I'm trying to get a jump start on the reading. You okay?"

Jan contemplated how much to tell her. She was

only a year and a half older, but Delaney worried and fussed like a grandma. Besides, any added stress always had the potential to trigger her eating disorder which had been under control for two years. And Jan didn't want to provide any reason for Delaney to quit her veterinarian tech courses. Again. Best to say nothing about the harassing phone calls or the near collision.

"Yeah. Guess who came to see me?" She related details of Marybeth's visit.

"You buried Bryan in your backyard? That's bizarre. Why'd she come up with that absurd notion now?"

"I have no idea. Especially since I had that tree planted months after he left."

"What do you think is going on with her?"

"I know she takes several medications." Jan crossed her legs and stroked Moxie who'd padded into the studio. "I asked about them and she nearly bit off my head."

"What does she take?"

"Don't know. Bryan said she'd been on meds for years, but never told me what she took."

"Her mood swings might indicate she's bipolar."

Jan sighed. "I agree. But I'm not going to ask again."

"What can you do?"

"Um," she paused. "There is something I can try. I'll talk to the new neighbor, Inez Nash. She's renting that little place around the corner. They seem to be very friendly. Next time I see her, I'll ask her to check on Marybeth. Make sure she's taking her medication."

"Do that, but keep away from Barnacle Buchanan, okay?"

"Easy for you to say. I have to drive past her house every day."

"You can always move."

"Don't start that again." Jan rolled her eyes. "Okay, time for *you* to go. Good-bye."

Jan ended the call and rested against the wall. Times like this, she missed their father's counsel most. She fingered the gold locket on its delicate chain—the last gift from him three years ago, given only weeks before their parents were killed in a car wreck. The palpable void loomed around Jan.

She missed her Heavenly Father's counsel, too. Sure, she attended worship services, but she used her busy schedule as an excuse to not get involved. In the past, she could pray at any time. However, her communication with God had dwindled to almost zero. Now would be a good time to reconnect.

Jan patted Moxie and closed her eyes. "Father, God, please help me..." Her voice cracked and she swiped at a lone tear.

CHAPTER 4

Hatch took the box of tissues off his desk and handed it to Tracy Taggart.

Giving him a weak smile, she yanked out a handful and wiped her eyes. "Sorry, Mr. Hatcher. I can't talk about my problems without crying."

Married at eighteen, two children before she turned twenty-one, and now old at twenty-six, Tracy stared at him through pain-filled dark eyes. Thirty minutes into the second session, she'd admitted Wendall, her husband, physically hurt her. Hatch had suspected as much after the initial visit although Tracy had indicated depression as her reason for coming.

Now her self-deprecating statements filled the office. "I'm a terrible wife. I can't do anything right. It's all my fault. If I didn't mess up, then everything would be okay."

Over the years, Hatch had seen the same scenario play out time after time. Physical and or verbal abuse eroded a woman's self-esteem, leaving behind a shell filled with hurt and grief. Tracy, the perfect example, cowered in the chair across from him. Few hurting women sought counseling. At least Tracy had returned for a second appointment.

Hatch's gut muscles tightened as her sleeve rode up, exposing discolorations on her forearm. Heavy makeup probably hid additional bruises on her face. Her left knee bounced up and down, a sign of the agitation seeping from her pores. Was she ready to take the next step?

"Let's discuss your options, Tracy. Have you ever called the police to file a complaint against your husband?"

Her leg stilled and she hung her head. "No. Wendall always says he's sorry."

Inwardly seething, Hatch tapped his pen on the pad. "He says that every time?" Another classic behavior described by most abused women.

She flinched and crossed her arms. "He *is* sorry, and I know he loves me. This time he didn't mean to punch me, but I forgot to buy his favorite beer."

"How long has he been hurting you?"

No response indicated the abuse had been going on for years.

"Have any of your injuries resulted in hospital visits?"

Again, no response.

Another question she probably wouldn't answer, either. "Does he force you to have sex?"

A faint blush tinted her cheeks.

"Is there anyone who can corroborate your accusations of him assaulting you?"

She frowned at him. "Why?"

Prepared for a hostile response, he grabbed the arms of his chair. "If you want to file charges against Wendall, evidence from a second party would go a long way in proving your case."

This time, she glanced at the door.

Don't leave yet, Tracy.

Purse held tightly against her chest, she slowly turned her head and looked at him and said in a soft voice, "My neighbor comes over sometimes after Wendall leaves the house. One time, she insisted on taking photos of my bruises and the broken bone poking out my forearm before she took me to the hospital."

Hatch nodded but fumed inside. "That's good." Keeping his tone even, he asked, "Why don't you want to file a complaint against Wendall?"

Tears pooled in her eyes and she tilted her head. "If he's arrested, won't he have a record?"

"Yes, but he'll know you're serious." Hatch adjusted his tie. "It might prod him to seek help or be willing to attend counseling sessions."

"I'll think about it."

"Another option is going to the Battered Woman's Shelter—"

"I can't do that."

"I understand it's a drastic step." Hatch glanced

out the window. Sun rays shot through the clouds in arrow-straight lines. He'd be a hero if solving Tracy's problems were that obvious. "Why don't you give them a call? Discuss your situation and get their advice."

A flicker of interest sparked in her eyes. She shifted in the chair.

He pressed on. "Do you want to call the shelter now?"

After twisting her silver wedding band, she shook her head. "I'll call later."

At least she acknowledged the possibility. Hatch gave her time to absorb her own words.

But with Sophie in mind, his next question ripped a piece off his heart. "Has Wendall ever lifted a hand to Olivia or Bobby?"

Tracy's eyes widened and her thin, pale lips quivered.

With his left hand balled into a fist, Hatch studied her body language. He'd worked with dozens of women in similar situations which had numbed him to some degree, but the urge to defend hapless victims lingered.

He repeated the question. "Has he?"

Sucking in a gulp of air, Tracy shook her head. "No." She stared at the floor, her upper body swaying from side to side. "He wouldn't hurt them, would he?"

How could Hatch answer? In his gut, he knew the chances Wendall would hurt his kids were statistically high. He locked onto her watery gaze. "Tracy, please listen. In my professional opinion, once a man crosses the line to beat his wife, he will beat his kids. Physical abuse is often preceded by verbal abuse. If you—"

"No. No." Tracy slumped forward, her hands covering her ears. "Don't say that. You don't know my Wendall. He'd never do that." She straightened and glared at Hatch, her tear-filled eyes asking the question her lips couldn't form.

As they sat in silence, Tracy seemed to provide her own answer. She lowered her head and heaved a sigh. "He does yell at the kids. Which scares them."

Hatch remained calm. "In the time we have left, we need to devise an action plan."

Plucking out another wad of tissues, Tracy wiped her eyes and blew her nose. Perched on the edge of the chair like a skittish bird ready to take flight, she sniffed and nodded.

"What I've told you hasn't been easy to hear, but you must face the possibility. Your children might be in harm's way. Contact the Battered Woman's Shelter for their advice. The next time Wendall loses control, call the police."

Seconds passed before she raised her head. A spark of resolve replaced the panic he'd witnessed earlier. She held his gaze. "Okay." Her knee bounced again. "Can I come see you again next week?"

"Sure." He hadn't scared her off. Hatch picked up his laptop from the side table and scrolled through his calendar.

They agreed on a date and time, but Tracy

hesitated to leave.

"Is there something else you'd like to discuss?" Hatch closed the computer and focused on the waves of fear, anxiety, and resolve flitting across her face.

"I don't understand how this system works. Will my husband find out I've come to see you?"

As an Employee Assistance Program network provider for the insurance offered by the call center where Tracy worked, Hatch was familiar with their requirements. Opening her file, he consulted the notes. "You listed your work address. Paperwork will be mailed there, and I certainly won't tell anyone."

After Tracy left, Hatch rocked back and forth in his desk chair. The human desire for revenge warred with his Christian principles. Violence was never the answer, but sometimes he wished he could pay back in kind what abusive men meted out. Tracy wasn't his only client in that situation, but she held a special place in his mind. She looked like Carol, his sister. And to help Carol, he'd sacrifice his life.

CHAPTER 5

Too confused by her conflicting emotions to concentrate, Jan set her sketchbook aside and drove to a nearby Chinese restaurant where she ordered Kung Pao chicken. Thirty minutes later, she returned home, ready to satisfy her tingling taste buds with the spicy food. Out of habit, she pushed the garage remote, but from the corner of her eye, she spotted a crimson advertisement hanging on the front door knob. Once parked, she grabbed her purse and lunch container. As she rounded the house and passed the living room window, a shot rang out. Searing pain stung Jan's forehead and she collapsed to the ground, careful to land on her side and not her back.

She lay still, in shock. Was she wounded? Hot liquid covered her forehead. She dabbed it with tentative fingers and examined them. Amber not red. Kung Pao sauce, not blood.

Slowly raising her head, she scanned the area. No visible threat.

Oscar Ortega, her neighbor, hobbled across the

lawn and knelt beside her, his cane abandoned in the flowerbed. "Are you hurt? My wife's calling the police."

Easing up, Jan sat cross-legged beside her lunch which lay splattered in globs all over the sidewalk. "My elbow's sore and something hit my forehead." She groaned as she wiped away more sauce. "It wasn't a bullet." *Thank You. Lord.*

"Sounded like a BB gun." Oscar adjusted his glasses and pointed to the house. "Could be the BBs ricocheted or hit the gravel and a piece flew up. You'd be bleeding for sure if hit by BBs."

"It stings." She took a tissue from her purse and wiped the goop off her forehead and fingers. "Do you think it could have been the Gimble twins? They're always up to no good."

Straining to stand, Oscar turned to the greenbelt across the street. "I'd bet on it. Oh, look. The police are here already. I'll talk to them." He retrieved his cane, limped across the lawn to two officers, and gestured toward the field, down the street, and then to Jan.

She closed the takeout container, her appetite for Kung Pao chicken as destroyed as her meal. Ants already formed a conga line to her spilled food. After standing and brushing dust and dried grass from her pants, she joined the officers and Oscar on the sidewalk.

"Ma'am, I'm Sergeant Voss. This is my partner, Officer Gonzalez. We were patrolling the area. Do you need medical attention?"

"No, thanks. I have a scraped elbow and a ping on my forehead." She rubbed the tiny dent.

They discussed the incident and the younger officer took notes.

"There's not much more we can do right now. We'll check out the kids' names you gave us and I'll let you know what we find out. We'll also check the open field across the street." Voss then examined the area where Jan had been walking. "I see BBs in the gravel. Gonzalez, gather them up."

While the officer placed them in a small plastic bag, Voss rested his hands on his thick duty belt. "If there's nothing else, we'll be leaving."

Jan did have something to tell them, but not in front of her helpful but nosy neighbor. She extended her hand. "Thanks for your help, Oscar."

He shook Jan's hand. "Glad you weren't hurt too bad. Better get on home. Flora will want to know what happened."

Jan waited until her neighbor reached his porch, and then she addressed the sergeant. "I do have something to discuss. Can we go inside?"

"Yes, ma'am. Lead the way."

Keys ready, Jan led them through the garage. "This is the door I usually use." She unlocked and opened it, then punched in the alarm code.

With the events of the previous evening fresh on her mind, she repeated the details of her earlier report.

"You have no idea where Bryan is?"

"No. If I did, I'd tell them."

"Who did you speak to last night?" Voss asked.

"A woman. I think her name was Franklin."

Gonzalez took notes.

"Did you get a license plate number? Make or model of the vehicle?"

"No. It was a dark sedan is all I recall. I didn't recognize the voice on either phone call." A flash of a memory buzzed around Jan's mind.

"Did Franklin ask for permission to check your phone records?"

She hesitated. "Yes…wait, I remembered something. I don't think the Gimble kids shot at me. When I pulled into my garage, I noticed a dark sedan parked across from Oscar's house. The…the shot came from that direction, sort of over my right shoulder. And when I joined you on the sidewalk, the car was gone. Did you notice it when you arrived?"

"There were only two light-colored cars further down. Do you think it's the same vehicle that drove menacingly toward you?"

"It could be." She folded her arms tight around her middle. "I wish these people would face me instead of threatening me."

"We'll do all we can to find out who's making the phone calls, but without details about the car, we—"

"I understand. Thank you, officers."

Voss nodded to his partner who opened the kitchen

door and walked through the garage.

"We'll be in touch." The sergeant stood by the door and turned to Jan. "I used to work with Teagan. She asked me to keep watch on you and Delaney. When your address came over the radio, I took the call."

"Sometimes it's good to have friends, or in my case, a sister, in high places. Thanks, again." Jan waited for him to exit the garage before punching the remote. Once safe inside, she reset the alarm and climbed the stairs. Losing herself in the sketches, the afternoon passed in a blur.

While nibbling on a microwaved meal, Jan remembered the mound of takeout she'd left on the sidewalk. She grabbed a handful of paper towels and headed down the hall. Carefully opening the door, she checked for any dark sedans parked in the street. None. The crimson advertisement on the handle that had drawn her attention that afternoon swayed in the breeze.

The front was blank.

She tugged it off and turned it over. Her blood froze. Printed in large black letters were the words: *I MADE YOU LOOK*

CHAPTER 6

Soon after Jan finished breakfast the next morning, Vince Mascorro, the New York publishing house art director called. "Hey, Vince. How much snow did you get this morning?" She'd worked with him for many years and often teased him about the northern winters.

"Don't sound so smug. Five inches."

"You should move to south Texas."

"Ha-ha. Like that's even a possibility. I don't have time to discuss the weather, kid. The deadline has changed. I need the preliminary sketches with accompanying prose next week."

"No problem. I'm almost done."

"Great. Send them as soon as you can. Gotta go."

Jan slipped the phone into her pocket and then shoved her sketchpad into her backpack. One more trip to the park today and she should have all she needed. Saturday would bring hordes of children out since the morning chill would quickly dissipate under the clear sky.

Dressed in a thick, black sweatshirt and blue jeans, Jan stood in front of the full-length mirror. She hadn't studied her reflection for a long time and didn't like what she saw. During the past year, she'd lost a lot of weight. Most of her clothes hung on her slender frame. Her shoulder-length honey-brown hair needed a trim and highlights. Moving closer to the mirror, she examined her pale skin and grimaced. "Ugh. You look older than Teagan." At thirty-five and eight years her senior, her eldest sister never appreciated the comments, but Jan and Delaney often teased her anyway. Her stressful job seemed to add years to her serious face.

Makeup would solve part of the problem for Jan. She applied foundation, especially to the bruise on her forehead, blush, and mascara. Pleased with the result, she gathered a jacket, her backpack, and a lapboard.

She activated the alarm and closed the door. A shiver scuttled through her body from scalp to toenails. Was a security system enough to keep her safe? Lying in bed the previous night she'd seen the crimson sign in neon every time she'd closed her eyes. What did it mean? Had it been placed on the door to get her in the right position to scare her with the BB shots?

Jan shook off the troubling thoughts and climbed into her SUV. She had work to do at Canfield.

Within ten minutes, she parked in the lot. Several children already occupied the playground equipment. Her main focus would be to capture their various body movements as they pumped the swings higher and higher, keeping in mind a sketch of the ferret would be added to one of the pages later. Seated on the same bench as before, she set her lapboard in place and opened her pad.

She added the finishing touches to the girl's outstretched legs and a gust of wind blew a sheet of paper off her backpack. Setting her pad aside, she scampered after it. Wisps of wind kept the paper floating up, up, out of reach. Then a man rose from the sandbox and snagged it.

"Here you are." He handed the paper to her. "Hey, the artist who helped Sophie."

Jan's stomach flipped when she recognized KC Hatcher. She took the paper and pointed to Sophie. "I see she survived the incident."

"Believe me, we had a serious discussion about playground safety, but since she's a few months shy of her fourth birthday, I'm sure we'll have the same discussion several more times."

Seeing him again tied Jan's tongue into a pretzel. She backed away, clutching the page, and stumbled into the bench. "Thanks again." She sat and placed the page inside her pad. Good thing the sketches were almost complete because her concentration had vanished. Jan's hands lay idle while her gaze drifted from the pad, to the swings, to the sandbox where Mr. Hatcher and Sophie constructed a large castle.

As if he knew her eyes were on him, he stood and

strolled toward her.

She quickly lowered her head, not sure how to unravel her muddled thoughts.

"Seems I've asked this before. Mind if I join you?"

Moving her backpack provided the seconds she needed to collect herself. "Please, sit."

"Friends call me Hatch."

"I'm Jan Sullivan."

"Is Jan short for Janet?"

"No, Janyth," she corrected.

"Janice."

"Janyth," she emphasized the last syllable.

"Sorry, Janyth."

"That always happens. Hardly anyone gets it right the first time. People usually think I have a lisp."

Sketching forgotten, she studied him. Broad shoulders under a navy-blue sweatshirt, windswept hair across his forehead, blue eyes wide and sincere, square jawline—

"…same problem."

Jan blinked. He'd been talking to her. "Pardon me. I didn't hear what you said. What problem?"

"My name usually gives me the same problem."

"What's wrong with KC Hatcher? Kevin Charles. Keith Cory."

"No, and no. You'll never guess the *K*." He squinted at her. "Are you a Bible scholar?"

She had been, years ago. "Sort of. Why?"

"Well, the *K* is for Keros and the *C* is for Caleb.

My parents were deep into Old Testament studies when I was born, hence Keros, and Caleb's my Dad's name."

"Keros. I don't remember reading about him."

"Check out—"

"No, don't tell me." Jan held up her hand. "I want to find it. I'll let you know when I do."

"Good." A slow smile crept across his face. "That means you'll be coming back here again."

The implication of what she had promised hit her. "I don't know if I'll be back."

"Oh, I'm sorry." He frowned.

Jan liked his reaction. "What I mean is, I've almost completed the sketches and may not need to visit the park again."

The frown eased off his brow. "I bought one of your books for Sophie. *Mr. Caterpillar Builds a House.* She loves it. Except she calls him Mr. Caterpeeper."

"How cute."

"I ordered the rest of the set for her birthday."

Why was he telling her this? She gave herself a mental thump. Don't blow it. Keep him talking.

"What kind of counselor are you?"

"Marriage and family, substance abuse, you name it."

He wore no wedding ring, but Jan had to know for sure. "Mrs. Hatch, what about her?"

Taking a moment to answer, he waved to Sophie in the sandbox. "Laura died when Sophie was eight months old."

"I'm sorry." Jan wanted more details but noted his pinched lips.

"It's okay. I still miss her, but we're coping."

Children's laughter, shouts, and squeals permeated the silence.

Then Sophie touched her father's knee. "Daddy, I'm hungry. Can we go now?"

He checked his watch. "I can't believe we've been here this long. No wonder you're hungry, honey. It's almost noon."

"That late? I must go too." Jan placed her sketchpad in her backpack.

Hatch took Sophie's hand and nodded to Jan. "You have my card. Call me when you find Keros in the Bible."

Laughing, Jan glanced sideways at him. She'd enjoyed the morning, and his honest blue eyes sent out positive signals. At least he hadn't hinted she needed his services this time. "I will."

In her vehicle, Jan hummed to a tune playing on the radio from the playlist on her smartphone. She couldn't believe she'd ascertained he didn't have a wife and had agreed to call him sometime. What was she thinking?

With Keros on her mind, she sat at a table in her favorite Italian restaurant and removed his card from her pocket. She expected the back to be blank so was surprised to find a picture of an old country church building and a statement. *If you're looking for a church home, visit Deer Park Community Church.* The address and website followed. An interesting proposition.

45

CHAPTER 7

As Hatch strapped Sophie into her car seat his cell phone rang. Caller ID named one of his clients.

"Hi, Mick. What's up?"

"I need to see you right away. Can't wait until Monday. Please, doc."

"Can you tell me over the phone?" Hatch had to remind clients time and again he was a plain Mister, but they often ignored his correction.

"No. Please, doc, I know it's the weekend but I need your help."

Hatch tried to reserve Saturdays for Sophie, but something in the man's desperate tone alerted his senses. "Fine. I'll meet you at my office in half an hour."

Before leaving the parking, lot he called his friend, Margaret who agreed to babysit. He drove to her house. "Sorry for the short notice. Would you mind giving her a sandwich?"

"No problem." She took Sophie's hand. "Let's see what sandwich fixings we have."

Hatch's meeting with Jan filled his mind as he hurried to the office. Janyth. Interesting name. Interesting occupation. Interesting lady. Would she search for the name Keros and would she call if she did?

When he arrived, Mick paced the sidewalk. They entered the office and emerged into the sunshine forty-five minutes later. After a quick handshake, Mick climbed on his motorbike and roared off.

Driving to pick up Sophie, Hatch reviewed the session, thankful he'd listened to his gut. Or was it his heart? Mick had recently separated from his wife. During a dispute about whose turn it was to have the kids, Mick became so angry he almost ended the relationship right there. Before he could say or do anything drastic, he'd called Hatch. By seeing Mick at this time, Hatch had helped the man cool off, and they'd been able to discuss his options rationally. Of all the cases Hatch counseled, the ones involving young children always rattled him the most. At least Mitch had never been physically abusive to his wife or kids. Not like Tracy's situation.

Parked in Margaret's driveway, Hatch heard his daughter playing in the backyard and he opened the gate.

"Hi, Daddy." She ran toward him. "Maggie's getting me juice."

Hatch picked up Sophie and planted a kiss on her forehead. "Had fun?"

"Uh-huh."

Margaret stuck her head out the kitchen door. "Problem solved?"

"For now." Swinging Sophie to his back, he carried her inside. "I'm glad I met with him. He was dealing with a serious situation."

"You're a good man, Hatch."

He cringed at her words of praise. Never had he felt more unworthy of anyone's admiration.

Margaret set another glass on the table. "Want some?"

"Sure." Picking up his drink, he saluted her.

"Did you eat?"

"No."

"Sophie insisted we make you a sandwich, too." Margaret removed it from the refrigerator.

"Thanks."

They sat at the kitchen table, enthralled by Sophie who managed to finish her juice while describing the antics of the neighbor's cat. She plunked her empty plastic cup in the sink and ran out the back door.

"She's a hoot." Raising an eyebrow, Margaret asked, "What's new? Sophie said you were at the park talking to a woman who was drawing."

Hatch took a bite of the roast beef on rye and again Jan's sad, haunted eyes dominated his recollection. What could he tell Margaret? He'd met an artist. She intrigued and interested him. There really wasn't much more to tell, was there? "We chatted while Sophie played in the sand."

"And that's all?"

"Yeah." Knowing she could see right through his nonchalance, he grinned. "For now."

Margaret teased him and begged for more detail, but he refused to indulge her.

"Thanks again for babysitting. I have piles of paperwork at home."

"You know I would do anything for you and sweet Sophie."

~*~*~

While Jan enjoyed her meal, friends from university days, Heather and Abigail, had entered the restaurant and Jan invited them to join her. An hour and a half later, she wound through the neighborhood on her way home and spied a parked maroon Jeep Renegade. Hatch drove a maroon Jeep. She'd taken particular notice. Meeting him again had added a glimmer of hope to her awakening heart. She wanted to find out more about him. Did he live there? She slowed in time to see him exit the house with a raven-haired woman and Sophie. He wrapped the woman in a bear hug and then held her hands.

Jan sped away, swallowing her disappointment.

CHAPTER 8

"Excuse me, ma'am, is this seat taken?"

Glancing up at the speaker, Jan shook her head. The large man plopped down on the pew beside her, and she scooted over to give him more room. She tried to concentrate on the words of the songs, prayers, and the sermon, but her thoughts warred within her mind. *Bryan and loss; Hatch and hope; Hatch and...nothing.* She had no reason to suspect he regarded her as anything more than an acquaintance, however, the memory of him hugging the brunette crushed her fantasy daydream.

After the last hymn, she made her way to the front doors, nodding to acquaintances, and greeting friends, all in a daze of distraction. Resolved to reach her car as quickly as possible, she brushed passed Marybeth and abruptly returned to earth. She pivoted, summoning the courage to speak to the woman and address their last meeting. Expecting rudeness or anger, instead, she found Marybeth's smiling face inches from her own.

"Come here, sweetie," purred Marybeth. "These

gentlemen want to meet you."

Jan's gaze flickered over the two tall, almost bald men dressed in dark suits standing with Marybeth. She tried to hide the utter surprise she knew must be plastered on her face. Marybeth was civil to her. What next?

"This is Jan Sullivan. She was my son's fiancée. Jan, this is Tom, and…what did you say your name is again? You'll have to forgive an old woman."

"Harold."

"Oh, yes. Harold." Marybeth beamed.

Jan could not believe the scene playing out in front of her. Courteous Marybeth. Flirtatious Marybeth.

"Hello, Tom, Harold. What can I do for you?" Something in their demeanor waved a warning flag, and Jan twisted her purse strap.

The men whispered to each other, and then either Harold or Tom—Jan couldn't tell as they looked so much alike—pulled Jan aside and slithered away from the crowd. Her escort's closeness gave her the creeps. She glanced over her shoulder at Marybeth who giggled at the other man.

They approached a railing protecting a hibernating flower bed, and Jan stopped. "That's far enough." She folded her arms. "Now if you don't mind Tom…Harold…"

"It's Tom, Ms. Sullivan. We're old college buddies of Bryan's and would like to contact him. Do you know where he is?"

Tom's question hit Jan like a Rocky Mountain avalanche. Already unnerved by phone calls and a close call in her SUV, any mention of Bryan sent her radar into high gear.

The image of Tom wavered before her eyes. Grabbing the railing with both hands, she drew in a ragged breath.

"Ms. Sullivan, are you all right? Did you hear my question?"

She nodded and turned, still grasping the railing. "Your question surprised me. Bryan left a year ago. I haven't seen him since, and I don't know where he is."

"Come now." Tom leaned against the railing. "Your fiancé left without a word?"

The anguish and turmoil she'd endured when Bryan disappeared gushed over her again. The hollow in her stomach grew. "I'm telling you the truth. He *did* just walk out on me."

"His mother thinks he's dead. What do you say to that?"

Jan squinted at him, then looked at Harold observing them closely. Marybeth, no longer fawning over the man, glared at her.

"Are you two responsible for the strange phone calls and for trying to run me off the road?" She didn't wait for a reply. "I have nothing else to say except I know Bryan's not dead." Jan stormed off to her SUV, zoomed out of the parking lot, and drove a mile or two before stopping along the curb in an unfamiliar neighborhood. Releasing her clenched hands from the steering wheel, she huffed out a breath. What to do? She wasn't hungry. Had no inclination to create anything in her studio. She needed comfort and normality. Ah-huh. A visit to Grandmother. Seventy-six-year-old Grandy Rachael lived in an upscale retirement community off Blanco Avenue in the north-central area of San Antonio. Grandy always provided a calming influence.

Jan checked the time as she headed east. Residents might still be in the dining room. If Grandy acted true to form, she'd be part of a group of friends, dawdling over their dessert and coffee. Jan signed in at the reception desk and then, sure enough, she found her grandmother at one of the large round tables near the windows. The Leander Hills Retirement Community occupied prized real estate surrounded by rolling hills covered in thick vegetation that accented the small man-made lake. Even in winter, the views from the dining room were spectacular. Jan didn't blame the residents for lingering.

Grandy waved a greeting. "Come join us, lovey. So good to see you. Do you want a piece of German chocolate cake or strawberry cheesecake?"

A waiter added another chair to the group, and asked, "Coffee, ma'am?"

"Yes, please, and a slice of cheesecake." Jan hugged Grandy, sat beside her, and nodded to the other five people at the table.

While sipping coffee and savoring the scrumptious cheesecake, she absorbed the energy from the group. They were planning an excursion to Corpus Christi the next weekend, and as usual, Grandy led the pack. They were known as Rachael's Rollators. Each one needed the wheeled assistance to walk safely, but nothing seemed to hamper their activities. One of the men owned a large SUV that could accommodate five passengers and their rollators. He drove and Grandy acted as copilot.

Plans completed, the residents left the dining room, and Grandy indicated Jan should follow her. "Walk me to my room, lovey, and tell me what's eating at you."

"I didn't come here to burden you with my problems."

"Nevertheless, talk to me, child." Grandy favored her left hip as she walked.

Jan and her sisters kept a keen watch on their grandmother's well-being since she'd received a hip replacement after a nasty fall eighteen months ago.

"Are you in pain?"

"No, no. Nothing to worry about. These old bones don't like the damp cold." She fluffed her pink-tinted silver curls.

In the elevator, Jan put her arm around her grandmother's shoulders. She'd always been slender, and despite the menu options, had not put on any weight during the year she'd lived at Leander Hills, her choice of accommodation after Grandfather passed away two years ago. She wanted her independence and wouldn't consider living with one of her granddaughters.

Grandy unlocked the door of her fifth-floor apartment. "Come in, but ignore the mess. I've been cutting out quilting squares." She set her rollator beside her recliner and sat, smoothing her wool skirt over her knees. "What's on your mind?"

After sifting through the jumbled chaos in her brain, Jan shared the basics with Grandy, omitting the phone calls and the meeting with Harold and Tom.

"My dear child. It's hard to believe Bryan's been gone a year, but remember, you are not to blame. You are a kind, caring person; his leaving is his loss. The road to happiness is never easy. I'm proud of how successful you are, and if you want a mate to share your life, you'll find him. In time."

Close to tears, Jan changed the subject and asked about the trip to Corpus Christi. Grandy expounded on the details of their overnight adventure. She asked after Delaney and Teagan, and thirty minutes later, Jan took her leave. Grandy never interfered in the lives of her granddaughters but would offer advice if asked. For this reason, Jan always enjoyed her visits and left with a more positive outlook.

However, when she climbed into her SUV and noticed her Bible on the passenger seat, the events at church that morning replaced the warm fuzzies Grandy inspired. Jan could understand—to some extent—

Marybeth's motives. After all, she had lost a son. He'd walked out on her, too. But Tom and Harold? Tom and Harry? Could Dick be far behind? Aliases, surely. And they were too old to have been Bryan's university buddies. Who were they and why come now, a year after he'd left? Were they responsible for the phone calls? So many questions, but no forthcoming answers.

While driving home, a car pulled out in front of her and she slammed on the brakes. Her Bible flew to the floor. At the next light, she retrieved it. A business card protruding from the pages marked the place where she'd found the name Keros.

She grabbed the card and fingered it, a tangible reminder there was life after Bryan. Hiking her shoulders as if to shake off the past, she took a quick glance at Hatch's headshot. Should she call him? Jan pulled into her driveway and waited for the garage door to open, placing the card on the console beside her. No. She wouldn't make that call, but given the strange meeting with Harold and Tom, and Marybeth's antagonism, it might be time for Jan to find a new church home. Deer Park seemed like a good option.

Jan worked on her final sketches most of the afternoon and added the last pencil strokes to the ferret as dusk settled. She spent the next hour pasting the typed script to each page then emailed Vince and advised him to expect her scanned pictures. He knew the paintings would follow as soon as the sketches were approved.

That night she had a strange dream. Bryan joined a group of her classmates from kindergarten. They sang the song that had brought Jan to tears so many times.

"Here comes Janyth, here comes Janyth.
She has a crooked back..."

Then Bryan stopped singing and poked her shoulder.

Opening her eyes, Jan blinked at the streetlight filtering between the blind slats. She *was* awake, but the poking persisted. She turned. Moxie kneaded her shoulder. Jan sighed and snuggled under the covers, but sleep eluded her as the bullying taunts echoed through her mind. Would she ever be free of the humiliating memories?

The year began with her wearing a back brace which limited her physical activity. Two months into the year, she had the initial surgery to attach the expandable rods to her spine, above and below the curve in the thoracic section. Every four to six months thereafter, she missed school again for the surgery to lengthen the rods. She couldn't feel them in her back, but she was conscious of their presence and feared that if she played too vigorously and fell, the metal would poke out and her classmates would have something else to tease her about.

Enough. Enough. Jan threw back the covers, slipped into her warm robe, and worked on one of a landscape series *La Casa de Colores* gallery had requested. After a while, she slid off the stool and glanced out the window. A shadowy movement caught her eye. She peered into her backyard. Illumination from the Ortega's back porch light exposed Sammy their dog prowling through her flowerbeds. Still unsettled by her dream and the strange events of the past few days, she backed away from the window.

She returned to her painting and although her enthusiasm had diminished, continued anyway. By morning, halfway through the series of paintings, she almost collapsed when fatigue and hunger took over. She showered, dressed, and ate a substantial breakfast. Four of the landscapes, done in acrylics, were ready to take to the art gallery. She carried them one at a time to the garage and loaded them into the custom-made rack in the back of her SUV.

At the gallery, Pat and Francisco Perez, owners of *La Casa de Colores*, greeted her with good news.

"Jan, *mija*, we sold three of your San Antonio River Walk scenes last week. Do you have any more? How are the landscapes coming along?"

"That's wonderful. I have several River Walk pictures at home, but I brought four landscapes with me today."

Francisco took Jan's car keys and within a few minutes, had carried in all the canvases.

Business details settled, Jan left the gallery and drove home. Despite still suffering from the effects of her long night, she returned to her studio to work on additional landscapes. Her energy soon waned. She added crooked siding to the barn and then abandoned the project.

While clearing away her supper dishes, Sergeant Voss called.

"We confirmed the Gimble boys were not in the area the day you were shot at, and the calls came from a burner phone. No help there. Has anything else suspicious happened?"

Closing the dishwasher, Jan frowned. Did meeting two creepy men count as suspicious? "No, sir."

He reminded her to be careful and ended the call.

Another dream, but this time a pleasant one, was interrupted by a melodious tune. Struggling to wake she didn't even check the screen and croaked, "Hello."

"It's Vince, and before you yell at me, I know it's early, but I have an assignment for you."

She blinked at the clock. "At six in the morning?"

"Yes. Love the sketches, by the way. Start painting, but we want the big tree dominating one of the scenes in more detail."

"The huge Live Oak?"

"Right. The whole tree with an old-fashioned rope swing hanging from a branch. You know, two thick ropes with Flossie on the wooden seat. We will use it as the cover. Okay?"

Sitting on the side of the bed, Jan stretched. "No problem. But couldn't you have waited a couple of hours?"

He made a kissing sound and hung up. Moxie narrowed her eyes at Jan as if disgusted at having her routine so rudely interrupted and jumped off the bed. Jan knew she could draw the requested picture freehand, but the desire to go back to the park and copy that magnificent oak took control of her sane thoughts.

Thirty minutes later, she slipped on her jacket and headed through the kitchen toward the garage. Rumblings in the heavens stopped her in her tracks. *Rain*? She peered out the window. Large drops splattered against the glass and within seconds, sheets of water blurred the scene.

Shoulders slumped, Jan returned to her studio. If the rain stopped at some point she could still go to the park. In the meantime, she began the sketch from memory, at least getting the basic outline down.

By early afternoon, the rain ceased, the clouds scattered, and Jan set off for the park. Moist, earthy smells lingered and sunlight glinted off the wet metal framework of the playground equipment. She chose a different bench where she could concentrate on the tree. Covering the damp wood with an old towel she kept in the car, Jan sat and enhanced the preliminary sketch until completely satisfied. Then she added the rope swing and Flossie on the seat and held the pad out in front of her.

"Another swing I'd like to try."

She jumped at the voice behind her and almost

dropped her sketch pad. "Hatch." She scanned the playground. "Where's Sophie?"

"I was on my way to pick her up from her daycare around the corner and noticed a pale green Chevy Tahoe in the parking lot and a woman on a bench. I thought it might be you."

Jan's brow furrowed in a mock frown. "Who else would be crazy enough to be sitting here after such a rain?" Her heart fluttered knowing he recognized her vehicle.

Grinning, he sat to inspect her picture. "Now you're doing illustrations for a book on trees?"

"No." She chuckled. "The art director asked specifically for this tree with a rope swing added. The other sketches have been approved. Now I can start painting."

They discussed the sketch then Hatch pointed to his watch. "Sophie's teacher will be wondering where I am."

"And I have to go, too."

Avoiding puddles and stepping over muddy patches, they walked to the parking lot. Hatch stood by Jan's car as she opened the door. She placed her backpack and lapboard on the passenger seat and couldn't help but see Hatch's business card on the console. "Keros is mentioned in the book of Ezra. I can't recall chapter and verse off hand, but I found it."

"Ezra 2:44. Good job."

Settled behind the wheel, she stared up at him.

He leaned in and spied his card. "Does this mean you won't need my business card any longer?"

She tilted her head. "I'd like to keep it if you don't mind." Why did she say those words?

"I don't mind at all. Especially if you call me anyway."

He winked, closed her door, waited for her to reverse, then walked to his car. All images of him hugging a woman vanished from her mind.

Negotiating twists and turns through the neighborhood, Jan sang along with a song from her favorite playlist. Waiting at a stoplight, she picked up Hatch's business card. She told him she wanted to keep it. She must be losing her mind.

Hatch had captured her attention. Not good-looking in a movie star way, but when he smiled, the dimple appeared, his eyes lit up, and she knew she could stare at him forever. *A bit over the top, Janyth.* It might have been her imagination, but she was sure she noted a spark of interest in his eyes before he'd winked and closed her car door.

Since Bryan's disappearance and abandonment, Jan had avoided close relationships. The encounter with Hatch had revived a part of her heart she thought had been numbed forever, but the risk of vulnerability lurked around every corner. She'd never had a long-term boyfriend, and then along came Bryan. They dated. He proposed. They planned a wedding, but he took off. Without an explanation.

Once home, she changed into painting attire and entered her studio. Surrounded by music from her MP3 Player, she set to work. She'd already purchased the cold-pressed paper for the illustrations. The special acid-free paper didn't buckle when saturated with watercolor paint. With the rope swing on her mind, she secured a fifteen-by-eleven-inch piece of paper to her special adjustable drawing board and copied the sketch from her pad. When satisfied with the rendition, she began the cover painting.

Absorption in her work kept Hatch in the distant recesses of her mind, but occasionally as wisps of paint stained the paper, butterflies tickled Jan's stomach when she anticipated what a phone call to him might bring.

She didn't have long to find out. Her cell phone rang. No name appeared on caller ID, and she experienced a moment of panic. Labeling the number of previous harassing calls as *Crank* was of no use since Sergeant Voss reported they were made from a burner phone. Squaring her shoulders, she answered.

Hatch. A pleasant surprise, but she was curious. "How did you get my cell number?"

"I checked your website. You certainly are talented. How are you today?"

Checking her website could be construed as interest, but she still hesitated. "All right, thanks." They'd seen each other minutes ago at the park.

"That's good."

Now it seemed to be his turn to hesitate. "Um…"

"Hatch, why did you call?" Was he trying to build up the courage to ask her on a date? Tingles rose from her toes to her heart.

"Well, blame it on my years of experience, but I sense you've been through or are going through a hard time. I meant what I said the first day we met. Let me know if I can help in any way."

Hinting she needed therapy certainly squelched the date notion. "I'm not sure what's going on here. I admit I've had a rotten year, but I don't need counseling. Thanks for your concern."

"Okay, but remember, talking about problems with a professional is important to healing."

Jan sat on the stool and scowled at her phone. What a nerve. "Thanks, Mr. Hatcher. I have your number in case I change my mind. Goodnight." She folded her arms and stared at the painting on the board. Swings suddenly lost their mystique.

CHAPTER 9

The next day, hunger pangs forced Jan to consider the contents of her refrigerator. When she didn't find anything substantial, she drove to a strip mall and stopped at the corner bistro for lunch. She enjoyed the Rueben sandwich and side salad and beckoned the waitress for the bill.

Crossing the parking lot, she noticed a familiar man walking ahead of her. Hatch. She didn't want him to see her and slowed her steps, but the mere sight of him in jeans that hugged his muscular legs sent heat scampering to her face. His recent annoying phone call all but disappeared from her memory.

He dropped a small paper sack, picked it up, and turned. "Jan, hi."

"Hello." She struggled to keep her tone even.

"What brings you out on such a cold day?"

She pointed to the bistro. "Lunch."

"Me, too. The Thai restaurant a few stores down."

"I need to leave." She continued walking and he stayed by her side. "How's Sophie?"

Pride shone from his eyes and coated his voice as he gave her a rundown of his daughter's latest exploits.

When they reached her car, Hatch said, "I'm parked in the next row. Bye."

She watched him for a second or two and then pressed the remote but didn't open the door.

The front tire was flat.

"Drat!" She squatted to examine it. Jagged gaping wounds glared at her. Who could have slashed her tire? Jan straightened and glanced at the vehicles around her. No other tires had been cut. A cold gust flicked a strand of hair across her face. She shivered. Not because of the wind, but because of a sneaky suspicion that snaked into her heart. Were Harold and Tom to blame?

Popping the liftgate, Jan released the rack for her canvases from its tether, moved it aside, and grabbed the owner's manual, thankful her father had insisted his daughters knew the basics of changing a tire. However, the directions provided were more complicated than simply lifting the load floor flap and locating the spare and the jack. Even if she followed the instructions, removing the tire would strain her back. Jan set down the book and pulled out her phone. Why pay for roadside assistance and not use it?

"Need a hand?"

She spun around and swiped at a strand of hair that impeded her vision. "You could say that. How did you know?"

Hatch shrugged. "Before I got in my car I took one

last peek at you."

"I'm glad you did."

"Where's the spare?"

"Under there." She pointed to the rear bumper. "The jack's in the side panel, and you need a key." She handed him the manual. "See for yourself. But I can call for roadside assistance. I'm sure they'll be here by the time you've read the instructions."

He scanned the pages and then chuckled. "Certainly not as straightforward as my Jeep. But I can manage."

Hatch followed the directions and removed the spare, the jack, and the tools. He rested the spare against the fender and pointed to the slashes. "What happened here?"

"Wrong place, wrong time, I guess." Her cheeks burned, but not from embarrassment this time.

"Somebody sure took a dislike to your tire. Did they only slash one?"

The blood fled from Jan's face, leaving her light-headed, but she dashed to the other side of the car and checked the tires. They were whole. "Yeah."

She wiped her forehead and watched Hatch work. Waiting for assistance might have taken hours, but he accomplished the task in a few minutes. He stashed away the tools and dumped the slashed tire in the cargo area.

"Your car is ready, madam." He grinned and opened the door.

"Thank you, kind sir. And I really mean that." Jan slid into the driver's seat.

A dimple teased his cheek as Hatch doffed an imaginary hat. "Have that tire repaired, and remember my offer. Take care."

An arguing couple in the next row of vehicles caught his attention and the smile slipped from his face.

Intrigued by the abrupt change in Hatch's expression, Jan also watched the couple. The short, skinny man jabbed his finger in the woman's face, yelling expletives, then stormed off to a liquor store. The woman followed like a bedraggled puppy.

Without another word, Hatch turned and walked away.

Jan sighed and glanced in the mirror. A black streak stretched from her eye, across her cheek to her chin. "Nooo," she groaned.

CHAPTER 10

Driving to his office, Hatch's fingers vise-gripped the steering wheel. He'd recognized Tracy and the man arguing with her was probably Wendall. Hatch could hardly comprehend the venom in the man's tone as he spewed hateful words to his wife. But his behavior fit the stereotypical abusive spouse. Hatch wondered if Tracy would make it to her appointment the next day.

He turned into the office complex, shoved the parking lot scene off to a far corner of his mind, and focused on Jan. Her initial demeanor toward him had been cool, but their meeting underscored his original opinion. Spunky, but with feet solidly planted in reality. He'd paid special attention to her eyes. The haunted look had been replaced by a spark of interest—that sent a smile to his lips—but also a hint of something dark. Like fear, maybe. He needed to get her to open up.

Slashed tires didn't just happen. Someone had it in for her. While changing the tire, he'd noticed security cameras mounted on the light poles. The malicious deed could have been filmed. A call to Garret Emerson, his private investigator buddy, might be in order. Even if the footage led nowhere, Garret could locate the slimiest of bad guys. And Hatch had no doubt someone slimy was responsible.

He arrived at his office with a few minutes to spare. Unlocking the door, he straightened the magazines on the coffee table, righted a cushion on the sofa, and stared into the small oval mirror above it. He wanted his clients to feel at ease so he often wore semi-formal attire. A button-down shirt and tie even with blue jeans. Adjusting the knot of the navy stripe, he gave

himself the once over. Did Jan like what she saw? He hoped he hadn't been mistaken in the glimmer of attraction he'd noticed.

A knock at the door. "Hi, Mr. Hatcher. Am I early?"

Turning, he smiled. "Right on time. Come on in." He guided the client to his inner office and closed the door. His rack of business cards sat precariously close to the edge of his desk. He moved it. Cards. Jan wanted to keep his. The way she tilted her head and smiled. That memory would last him a long time.

CHAPTER 11

During the rest of the week, Jan slogged away at the paintings for the book and only left her house once. First, she took her car to the dealership and bought a new tire which they installed. Excitement over how well the pictures were turning out overcame any residual anger she had regarding the tire-slashing incident.

Eager to return to her studio, she hurried through the grocery store and purchased a selection of frozen meals. On the way home, she stopped at Supreme Art World, the wholesale art supply store she frequented. She preferred to use watercolor paints in tubes and needed another titanium white. Her well-stocked cabinet had revealed a tube of the paint, but it had a small hole at the base and the paint had dried out so much, it was unsalvageable.

The art store shared a parking lot with Abel's, a large DIY center. On the way back to her vehicle, she noticed Hatch walking arm-in-arm with a redheaded woman. They laughed together and seemed to be having a great time as they entered Abel's. Jan's steps slowed. Hmm. Raven-haired woman last week and a redhead this week. Hatch seemed to be a popular guy.

Pressing the remote, Jan opened her car door and shrugged. His personal life had nothing to do with her. However, she was glad she'd met him. Her physical attraction to him was a positive sign. At least she wasn't dead inside. But she had pictures to complete and had no time to dwell on Hatch.

She drove home and upon entering her kitchen, dumped her purchases on the counter. Groceries packed away, she set a container of chicken enchiladas in the microwave, then poured food into Moxie's bowl. Usually, the sound of nuggets hitting the metal container was the cat's dinner gong. But no ball of fluff appeared. Jan scanned the den, living room, and dining room, then ran upstairs and called again, checking each room.

"That's strange. Where can she be?"

Calling constantly, Jan returned to the kitchen and opened the sliding glass doors leading outside. The spoiled cat hated the cold weather and only spent the briefest few minutes outdoors. Jan crossed the patio and inspected the sage bushes along the fence. No cat hiding behind them. No Moxie anywhere.

The only other possibility was Moxie entered the neighbor's yard through the gap their dog had dug under the fence. Jan called the cat again. By now the tingle of unease in Jan's stomach increased. Moxie had never left the yard before and she was not a fan of Sammy. Jan opened her gate and ran to the Ortega's front door. When Oscar responded to her knock, she asked, "Have you seen Moxie?"

"No—"

Jan pushed past him. "Please, can I check your backyard?"

"Of course." He followed her.

The search of the yard proved fruitless.

"Thank you, Oscar. If you see her…"

"*Sí, sí.* I will keep Sammy inside in case Moxie comes here."

Back in her kitchen, Jan stood beside the sink. If the cat didn't come home soon, she'd notify the Homeowners Association. They could email everyone in the neighborhood. Her stomach growled but she had no appetite. She set the container of heated lasagna on the counter and her phone rang. Taking it from her pocket, she checked caller ID. No name appeared but she couldn't let every call go to voicemail. She answered, "Hello, Jan Sullivan speaking."

A high-pitched voice, not muffled like on the previous prank calls, said, "Hi, Jan. I like your cat. I sent you a picture."

She threw down the phone as if it were on fire. After a few halting breaths, she retrieved it and looked at the photo. Moxie lay curled up in a cat carrier.

Close to tears, Jan called Teagan but had to leave a message. Her distress must have coated her words because her sister called back within minutes.

"What's going on, baby sis?"

Jan always fussed at Teagan for calling her the baby, but now the words comforted her. She related the recent events—threatening phone calls, the near miss with the car, and now Moxie. "What should I do?"

"First, send me the photo of Moxie and the names of the offices you reported to. Do you have any idea who might be doing this?"

How could she have forgotten? Jan disclosed the strange meeting with Harold and Tom and their interest in Bryan's whereabouts.

"Marybeth introduced them to you?"

"Right."

"I can't visit you right now, but I know Sergeant Luke Voss. I'll ask him to interview Marybeth and to get descriptions from you." She clicked her tongue. "You're too trusting, Jan. Why didn't you connect Harold and Tom with the phone calls? Weren't they after the same thing?"

"Give me a break. I don't have a cop's brain."

"Sorry. I know. Be careful. I have an idea—why don't you move into my place for a while? You'll have the condo to yourself. Think about it. I have to go. Bye."

Slumped on a chair at her kitchen table, Jan rubbed her temples. What a mess. Of course, Harold and Tom were involved. She stared at the photo of Moxie again. To get her cat back, she'd probably have to produce what the men were after—the location of Bryan or return whatever item they were after. However, she had no information about either option.

Back in the studio, she worked on the paintings for the book. Vince wanted them as soon as possible, no matter what chaos affected her personal life.

Later that afternoon, Sergeant Voss and Officer Gonzalez came to take her statement and to get descriptions of Harold and Tom.

"Did you already visit Mrs. Buchanan?" Jan rubbed her temple where a headache churned. "Did she have any information about the men?"

"No. She wasn't cooperative at all. In fact, she got downright hostile and professed not to know the men."

"Her reaction doesn't surprise me." Jan told Voss about Marybeth's recent odd behaviors. "She might not be taking her prescribed medications. I'm going to ask a neighbor to check on her."

"Good idea. In the meantime, there's not a lot more we can do. We'll circulate the descriptions you gave us." He turned to his partner. "Wait for me outside, please." After Gonzalez left the house, Voss continued. "Gonzalez doesn't know about Teagan. I'll share what I have with her. Your sister would be here if she could."

"I never expect to hear from her when she's on an assignment, but I'm glad she returned my call this time."

"I'm sorry about your cat. When the catnappers

contact you, be sure to let me know."

"I will. Thanks for coming."

Jan closed the door behind him and set the alarm. She paced the kitchen, phone in hand in case she received a ransom call.

Three times around the table and she'd had enough. She made herself a cup of hot tea and climbed the stairs to her studio. Seated at the counter, she set the phone down but picked it up immediately for one more look at poor Moxie. Jan enlarged the photo and frowned. A hand, a woman's hand she'd not noticed before, rested on a corner of the carrier. She leaned closer. Yes. The index finger was much shorter than it should be and had no nail. Just like Delaney's. A childhood injury she was no longer embarrassed by.

Fingers shaking, she dialed Voss's number and when he answered, said, "I know where my cat is."

CHAPTER 12

Ignoring Voss's instructions to stay home, Jan drove to the address of Delaney's house-and-pet-sitting job. When she arrived, police vehicles were already outside the large house, pulsating red and blue lights announcing their presence to the neighbors. Officers swarmed around the gardens and light blazed from almost every window.

An officer waved her to the side of the road, leaned forward, and indicated she should lower her window.

Jan did but spoke first. "My sister's in that house and she's in trouble. Is Sergeant Voss here?"

Voss hurried to her SUV before the officer could respond. "Miss Sullivan, I told you to stay home."

"How did you get here before me?" She peered around him at the house. "Is Delaney all right?"

"You'd better come inside." He opened her door.

Shoving her cold hands into her pockets, she followed him along the circular driveway to the front porch.

He pulled her aside. "You're not the only person

who noticed the hand in the photo. Teagan almost broke cover to call me and provide this address. Delaney is safe."

Delaney always provided her sisters the addresses of where she worked.

"Can I go inside now, please?"

"Of course."

Delaney sat on a leather sofa in the living room huddled under a blanket and talking to an officer. Dogs yapped from a far-off location.

Jan sat beside her, drawing her into a hug. "Are you okay? Did they hurt you?"

She shook her head. "Only scared me. When they noticed my short finger, they insisted I put that hand on the carrier for the photo, then they tied me up and…and…"

"It's over now, Laney." Jan turned to Voss who stood behind the sofa. "Did you find my cat?"

Her sister answered, "Moxie's fine. We were in the same bedroom. She's not hurt as far as I could tell. That's how they got in. A man showed me your cat in the carrier and said you needed me to take care of her as you were having your house fumigated." She harumphed. "I let them in. I should have realized—"

"Hey, you're safe and that's all that matters right now."

"I'm tired." She rested against the plush cushions and closed her eyes.

"The cops will be gone soon but I'll spend the

night with you." Jan eased up, glanced at Voss, and tilted her head toward the kitchen.

He followed her. "Teagan had already notified me, so by the time Delaney managed to free herself and call 9-1-1, I was en route. She let me in and described what happened. Initially, only one man wearing a cap low on his forehead stood at the front door. He held the carrier and gave her the spiel. As soon as she let him in, he pulled on a ski mask and another masked man entered behind him. Both wore gloves. They tied her up and left her in a back bedroom. I think they intended for her to get free. She said the rope was not very tight."

"Harold and Tom?"

"Possibly."

"Sergeant Voss, we're done. I'll meet you at the patrol car." Gonzalez nodded to Jan and Voss and left the house.

"Is there anything else I can do for you before I leave?" Voss asked. "Gonzalez walked the dogs in the back yard and now they're in the laundry room. The owners' cat is in the master bedroom, and your cat is in the first bedroom down the hall. We've taken the carrier and the rope to test for fingerprints."

"Delaney might seem to be handling the trauma well, but I'll spend the night anyway. Do you know her history?" Jan shook her head. "Never mind. I don't want to leave her alone, but I need cat food. For medical reasons, Moxie has special food and must eat regularly." Jan removed cash from her billfold and provided the brand of cat food.

"I'll take care of it."

"Thanks."

"And I'll let Teagan know what happened."

After the last police car drove away, Jan let out the dogs. The two Pomeranians headed straight for their padded bed beside the fireplace. She made two mugs of hot tea, gave one to Delaney, and then went in search of her poor cat.

Moxie, as calm as ever, lay curled up on the pillows. She raised her head and blinked. Jan carried her into the kitchen and gave her a bowl of water.

"Hey, sis. We don't need to tell Grandy about this…this event. She worries too much."

"I agree." Jan thought for a moment. "She's packing for her trip to Corpus Christi with her rollator buddies. No need to upset her."

"One of the men took my phone then removed my glasses and blindfolded me. Can you look for them, please?"

"Sure. I'll call your number." She followed the melodic tune into the laundry and located the phone and glasses in the dryer. A piece of paper was wrapped around the phone. Not something Delaney would do. A note from the catnappers?

Hands trembling, Jan removed the paper and unfolded it. Yep. A note addressed to her.

Jan, see how easily we can mess up your

life. Tell us where Bryan is or
     give us the items he stole. Don't share this
with the police. If you do,
     not only will your cat suffer, but so will
your sister.

The doorbell rang. Her blood running cold, Jan hurried to the living room and checked the peephole. Seeing Voss, she opened the door.

He handed her a shopping bag. "Cat food and a couple of chicken sliders. In case you're hungry and don't want to cook."

"Thanks for your thoughtfulness. Goodnight." She closed the door before the contents of the note burst from her mouth. Slowly entering the living room, Jan forced a smile as she handed her sister the glasses and phone.

"Now everything won't have fuzzy outlines." Delaney adjusted the glasses and then patted the seat beside her. "Come, sit. I appreciate you spending the night." She sipped her tea, cradling the mug with both hands. "This whole day has been an ordeal. I'm glad we're all safe, but I'm really ticked off. Yesterday, was the first day of term for me. One of the teachers was at the college before, you know three years ago when I dropped out. Mrs. Ingram remembered me and said, 'You're back.' There was no welcome in her statement. I missed her class today. How am I ever going to convince her I've changed?"

Jan sat on the sofa scrunching the piece of paper in her pocket. Missing a few classes would be the least of Delaney's worries if Jan divulged the contents of the note.

CHAPTER 13

"**And then my** new boss gave me a stack of papers to file, and it was already four o'clock, and I hadn't even run the copies yet."

Hatch stopped at a red light and attempted to focus on his companion's constant chatter, but his head was so full of jumbled words there wasn't room for one more. His stuffed brain also affected his speech, because all he could muster was an occasional, "Oh, really." Or, "Is that so?"

At Eva's destination, he escorted her to her front door, said goodbye as politely as he could, and sprinted back to the car. He drove away and vowed he would be very choosy in the future as to what little favors he did for Margaret. Helping her friend Eva select flooring for her new house was one thing. Accepting a "thank you" date for dinner—at Margaret's insistence—was completely different.

He arrived home and found Margaret, who was babysitting Sophie, in the kitchen removing cookies from a cooling rack and stacking them in the cookie jar.

"You're back early. Have a good time?"

"Well," Hatch tried to think of something positive to say. "She's a sweet person, but—"

"Did she talk your ears off?"

Folding his length into a chair, he glared at Margaret. "You knew?"

"Oh, Hatch." Giggles bubbled between her words. "You should see the expression on your face."

His grin eased into laughter. "Maggie, how could you? I don't think Eva tasted a thing she ate. She talked through the whole meal, and I couldn't get in a word sideways, edgewise, or up-side-down." He took the cookie she handed him. "Mmm. Oatmeal raisin."

"Eva appreciates your help. She recently moved to San Antonio and is lonely. Going out with you was probably the highlight of her month."

"No more, Maggie, please." Between bites of the cookie, he added, "Introduce her to some of your other friends."

"Hi, Daddy." Sophie ran into the kitchen. "Are they good? I helped Maggie make them."

"Hey, honey." He munched on the rest of the cookie. "You know they're my favorite and that one was the best cookie I've ever had." Hatch hugged Sophie and then turned to Margaret. "Thanks for taking care of my princess."

"No problem as usual. I love the little tyke."

Sophie helped Margaret stack the last of the cookies in the jar. She stood beside Hatch still sitting at the table. "Daddy, come to the backyard with me, please. I want to show you something."

"Can it wait until Maggie goes home?"

"I suppose." She skipped down the hall toward the living room.

Hatch and Margaret cleaned up the kitchen.

"I need to go home. Work is piling up." She gathered her coat and purse and headed to the front door. "Seriously, thanks for helping Eva."

Hatch rolled his eyes. "I think you owe me big time."

Grinning, Margaret buckled her seatbelt. "I'll do whatever you want."

He returned to the kitchen where Sophie waited with her coat buttoned and an impish smile on her sweet face.

"Daddy, come look," she pleaded as she opened the back door.

"What is it, honey?" He turned on the floodlights and followed Sophie to a massive oak close to the back fence. Its bare branches splayed like giant hands grabbing at the gray evening sky.

"Can you make me a swing in this tree? Please, Daddy, can you?"

He studied a large sturdy branch and remembered the picture Jan had been working on in the park. *A rope swing. That would work.*

"I think I can, honey. Give me a week or so, okay."

"Thanks, Dad." Sophie skipped down the path

singing, "I'm getting a swing, I'm getting a swing."

Hatch smiled at her enthusiasm then looked back at the tree and instead of bare branches, he envisioned the rope swing Jan had drawn. He stuck his hands into his pockets and stepped away from the tree. The swing swayed back and forth, back and forth, until he stumbled on the edge of the path, and the swing disappeared, leaving the tree branch bare again.

Back in the kitchen, he removed another cookie from the jar. An odd sensation rumbled in the pit of his stomach and it had nothing to do with imaginary swings. He wanted to help Jan, but he'd sensed her cooling attitude, and attributed it to his offering that help. At this moment, Jan as a friend was more important than Jan as a client. He'd back off and keep his opinions to himself.

If only his advice was as easy to follow as it was to give.

CHAPTER 14

Shoulders hunched against the cold evening air, Jan hurried to her SUV. She set Moxie on the back seat where she seemed quite at home. Despite the circumstances, Jan had spent a delightful day with Delaney. They'd given the owners' pets plenty of attention, had gone shopping, and even cooked a three-course meal for lunch. Jan learned a few tips from her sister who'd always had a knack for making tasty food without a recipe. No one would want to sample anything Jan created in the kitchen unless she'd followed directions and even then…

Although the threat in the note she'd received lurked behind every activity she'd engaged in during the day, Jan was confident she hid her apprehension well.

To keep the conversation on any topic but the previous day's events, Jan had mentioned her desire to leave Hillside Avenue Church and try a smaller congregation.

"You've been going there for a long time. Why

change now?"

"I haven't been completely satisfied at Hillside for a while."

"Because…"

"In my opinion, worship services there have become entertainment. Those of us in the pews sit back and listen to the choir. Sometimes we're encouraged to join in the singing, but so many songs are new, we don't know the tunes and are hesitant to join in. Mood lighting makes the auditorium feel like a theater."

"Are they teaching the truth?"

"They read from the Bible, but many sermons remind me of the Scripture that warns us to be wary of teachers who only say what itching ears want to hear. Something like that."

"Yeah, it's in II Timothy, I think chapter four."

"On the other hand, I don't want to attend a church where every message is a rebuke." Jan hung her head. "I will admit that I've allowed my busy life to erode my relationship with God. I can't blame it all on Hillside."

Delaney leaned closer and patted Jan's arm. "Believe me, I know what you're going through. When I was dealing with anorexia, I felt a thousand miles from God. But in reality, he was a mere step away. You, Teagan, Grandy, and Emily gave me the strength to face my problems and to reach out my hand to God." She twirled a strand of sandy-brown hair between her fingers, a gesture she'd picked up in childhood. "It wasn't easy."

"We're so proud of you, sis. None of us know the depth of your struggles."

"Hey, enough about me. What else is making you consider leaving Hillside?"

"The most important reason is seeing Marybeth Buchanan regularly. She overstepped the bounds by making those accusations last week, and I can't endure much more."

"I don't blame you."

Jan stroked Moxie who lay stretched out on the sofa beside her. The owners' cat, a cream-colored Persian, with dark ears, paws, and tail was probably in one of the bedrooms. "My heart will ache to leave a place where I enjoyed many years of fellowship." Not to mention that's where she'd met Bryan and where she hoped to be married. She lifted her gaze to the vaulted ceiling. "It's time for a change."

"Where will you go instead?"

Jan stood and stepped to the fireplace where the dogs slept in their bed. "I heard about a small community church close to my home. I think I'll go there tomorrow." And see Hatch? "Would you like to come with me?"

"No, but thanks for asking. Emily and I like the small congregation where we worship."

While cleaning up the kitchen, Jan had shared the interactions she'd had with Harold and Tom. Naturally, Delaney asked if she'd contacted Teagan.

"Of course. She knows Sergeant Voss and he can

communicate with her easier than we can."

"Do you think those men came here yesterday?"

"I told Voss I thought so."

Delaney placed an arm around Jan's shoulders. "Do you have anything of Bryan's?"

"No, and I certainly don't know where he is."

Later in the afternoon, they'd taken the little dogs for a walk, and Jan used the distraction to have a lengthy discussion with Delaney concerning the college teacher she'd had years ago. Jan ended the conversation with advice. "Show Mrs. Ingram you're not the person you were back then. Prove to her you'll work hard to complete the coursework for this associate degree. Find out from a classmate what was covered yesterday, and if you have to, explain to the teacher why you missed the class. I'm sure Sergeant Voss would be happy to give you a note."

That brought a smile to Delaney's face. "Thanks for reminding me I'm not the same person. I'll handle it like a mature adult and won't need a note."

"I was kidding about the excuse."

"I know." She chuckled. "I can see the expression on Mrs. Ingram's face and hear her response. 'You brought a note, Sullivan. Is it from your *mama*?'"

Before Jan left, she and Delaney agreed to text each other morning and evening, at least for the next few days. Satisfied Delaney would not relapse, Jan drove home. Her sister had coped with the whole episode much better than Jan had anticipated. *Thank*

You, God.

While she heated lunch leftovers for supper, Moxie strolled through the kitchen as if checking everything was in its familiar place. She stopped at the closed pet door and glared at Jan. "Sorry, Moxie, you have to get used to slumming it by using a litter box." Harold and Tom, the probable catnappers, would not be able to steal her cat again. Jan tapped her fork on the plate. The names Harold and Tom gave them too much legitimacy. In the future, she'd refer to the men as…The Thugs.

Her cell phone rang, and the familiar sound set her teeth on edge, but she relaxed when Sergeant Voss's name appeared on the screen. "Any news?"

"Sorry, no. There were only smudged fingerprints on the cat carrier, and the rope was old, a common type."

"Tomorrow, I'll ask Marybeth if she knows anything else about the men."

"We tried. Remember?"

"Yes, but I need to discuss an unrelated topic with her and will introduce the names at the right moment."

"Keep me informed. And take care."

Jan frowned as she shoved her phone into her pocket. Sure, keep him informed, but not when doing so would endanger Delaney's life. She headed upstairs and stood in her studio. Teagan's offer for her to move in sounded like a possible plan, but the thought of packing her vast supply of painting materials was worse than dealing with threatening phone calls. And notes. Which reminded her to text Delaney, who responded that all was well.

With a fresh canvas on the easel, Jan prepared a palette of acrylic paint. No landscape, playground equipment, or ferrets in mind, she created abstract designs representing her jumbled thoughts. Why did The Thugs think she had anything of Bryan's? He left nothing in her house—except the items she told Marybeth he collected back in May. Jan knew what was in each closet and drawer. Her laptop only contained her files, the contents of which she knew. Bryan had taken his laptop with him when he disappeared, or at least it wasn't in his apartment. So when The Thugs contacted her, she'd have nothing to give them. Other than being vigilant when out and about, there wasn't much more she could do.

An outlandish idea popped into her head. She could invite them into her home and let them search for themselves. Maybe then they'd quit harassing her, and Delaney and Moxie would be safe.

Jan studied her creation. Certainly different from her usual realistic work. The abstract design contained swirls and patches of dark colors, but overall, it was pleasant to look at. She might hang it in her bedroom.

While she tidied up the studio, she reviewed her plans for the next day. Visit Marybeth, gauge her mood, and then subtly introduce the topic of Tom and Harold. Jan thumped the counter. She'd forgotten to ask Inez,

Marybeth's neighbor, to check if she was taking her meds. Another item to add to her agenda.

Not willing to let the previous day's episode and the threatening note stifle her daily life, Jan located her laptop and Hatch's card and entered the website for Deer Park Community Church. They met in a portion of a strip mall in Deer Park, a newer neighborhood north of the city. She added the address to the contacts on her phone. The idea Hatch might be in attendance sent a tiny spark to her heart. She breathed out a whooshing sigh. *Que sera sera*. Whatever will be will be—her mother's favorite Doris Day song.

She showered and readied for bed. A car engine revved outside her house. Not too concerned, she turned off her bedside lamp. The doorbell rang. Her breath caught and a cold shiver slithered down her spine. She peeked through the blinds. Residents' vehicles she recognized were parked along the curb. The bell rang again. No one she knew would visit this late, but it could be someone in need.

Tomorrow, she'd do as Teagan advised months ago and purchase one of those smart doorbells that sent a picture of the person ringing the bell to her phone. Grabbing the handrail for dear life, she climbed down the stairs, tiptoed to the front door, and peeked through the peephole. No one there.

In case it was a person needing assistance, she called out, "Who's there? Do you need help?"

No response. Considering all the strange and

threatening events she'd endured recently, she didn't open the door. Heart racing, she returned to her bedroom and cradled a pillow to her chest.

CHAPTER 15

For the second time that night, Sophie woke up and called for him. Hatch soothed her again and tucked Patches Panda under the covers with her.

"Did you have a bad dream this time, honey?"

Eyes closed, the child shook her head. "There was a…a man by my window. He made scratching noises."

"What?" Hatch repeated his query in a calmer voice. "What did you say, sweetheart?"

She opened her eyes and pointed to the window. "I 'member what you said last time. The wind was blowing a branch and it scraped the wall."

"That's right. Tomorrow, I'll get my chainsaw and cut that pesky branch off the tree." He swallowed. "What…about the man? Did you see him?"

"I think so."

"Where?" Drawing the details from her was harder than climbing Pikes Peak backward, but he didn't want to scare her with repeated questions.

Sophie sat up, threw off the covers, and stepped to the window. "I opened the curtain and saw his face.

That's when I called for you."

A person outside the window of the two-story house? Hatch yanked back the curtain, unlocked the window, and opened it. The screen was secure, and he noticed nothing untoward in the garden below illuminated by the streetlight. "I don't see him. Are you sure you saw a man's face?"

"I don't tell lies, Daddy. He didn't have any hair."

A little too detailed to be a fabrication. "I know you're an honest little girl. I believe you, honey. One more question. Why did you go to the window?"

"This time the scratching was different. It was…um, two quick scratches, then three long ones. Over and over. Like we practice in music class."

As if made deliberately? Hatch tried not to encourage her to sleep in his room, but he made an exception. "Do you want to sleep in my bed tonight?"

Her bottom lip quivered and she nodded.

He picked up her and the panda, tucked them into his king-sized bed, and sat beside Sophie until she drifted off to sleep.

Reviewing Sophie's remarks kept him awake. He returned to her bedroom. Several books from her shelf were on the floor. Certain they weren't there when he read to her that evening, he gathered them together and was about to place them back on the shelf when the cover of the top book caught his eye. And he chuckled. A bald man surrounded by children. A couple of weeks ago, he and Sophie had stopped at a neighborhood yard sale. He allowed her to select five picture books at fifty cents each. When he noted the bald man, he'd asked her why she chose that book.

"'Cause Grandpa has no hair."

True. His father had been bald for many years. Had Sophie looked through these books after he'd read her a bedtime story and the bald man pictured infiltrated her dreams? Whatever the reason, no man, bald or not, would enter Sophie's bedroom window. He'd install a security system as soon as possible.

CHAPTER 16

A smidgen of regret in leaving Hillside Avenue Church and the trepidation in trying something new, along with the threatening note contributed to Jan's restless night. However, she awoke in time to fix a real breakfast—a vegetable omelet—and took more care than usual with her clothes. A new bronze sweater and calf-length silk skirt with gold and bronze cascading swirls, and brown boots completed her ensemble.

She replied to Delaney's text, and then using the directions displayed on her phone, Jan soon reached her destination. Deer Park Community Church nestled between a florist and a bank branch. Jan entered through the glass doors and stepped into the small foyer where a young man welcomed her. He directed her to scattered seats available in the back rows. She squeezed by an elderly couple and sat down.

The words of the hymns were projected on a screen, and since she knew many of them, added her alto voice to the mix. The congregation was much smaller than Hillside Avenue, but there were enough similarities in the style of worship to allow Jan to participate wholeheartedly in the service. Buoyed by the experience, she hoped the change would be the catalyst to get her spiritual life back on track.

The pastor's message on forgiveness encouraged Jan to examine her heart. Convicted to change her attitude toward Marybeth, she resolved to speak to the woman as soon as possible.

After the service, she made her way outside, greeted by several people wanting introductions. A slight twinge of disappointment that Hatch wasn't among the crowd clouded her mind for a moment. She hesitated on the sidewalk, felt a tap on her leg, and looked down.

"Are you the lady from the park?" A child's innocent stare met hers.

Taking advantage of the situation, Jan said, "Yes, I am, Sophie. Where's your daddy?"

"Inside. I wait for him out here."

Sophie disappeared through the sea of legs and latched on to one in particular. She grasped a hand and pulled the man over to Jan. "Look, who's here, Daddy."

Hatch took Jan's hand in both of his. "It's so good to see you. Did the information on my card encourage you to come here?" He released her hand and picked up Sophie.

"Yes. Since I'm looking for a place to worship, thought I'd pay a visit." He didn't need to know all the reasons behind her search for a new church.

"Great." He squinted against the bright sunlight. "I added the details about the church a couple of years ago."

"I'm glad you did. If you recommend the church, then it must be a good place. You have honest eyes."

His frown surprised her. He shifted Sophie on his hip, and said, "Care to join us for a potluck lunch? It's the preacher's birthday and his favorite food is chili."

Jan opened her mouth to respond but a woman approached Hatch.

"You were late today. I hope nothing's wrong."

"I don't want to talk about it." Scowling, he turned to Jan. "Jan Sullivan, this is Margaret Dawson. She'll take you to the social room if you want to stay." Hatch nodded then moved through the throng with Sophie in his arms.

Jan recognized Margaret as the woman she'd seen Hatch hug a week ago. Margaret wore a powder blue jacket over black pants. Her blue eyes, enhanced by the color of her jacket, held an icy stare. Of above-average height with short black hair and a creamy complexion any cosmetic model would envy, the woman radiated self-confidence.

Her insecurities forgotten for a moment, Jan said, "Nice to meet you. Have you attended here long?"

"Yes. How do you know Hatch?" A hint of jealousy dusted the words.

"I met him and Sophie at the park." Jan scribbled a mental note to thank Delaney for suggesting she purchase her skirt and sweater, a vast improvement over her usual blue jeans. For once, she didn't feel inferior in the company of a confident beauty.

"The artist. Yes, Hatch mentioned you. He's always collecting strays." She gave Jan the once-over then tilted her head."

Jan held up her chin and squared her shoulders.

"Come this way." Margaret led her into a large room with round tables, chairs, and people milling around.

Savory aromas swirled toward her. Crock pots, probably filled with chili, and casserole dishes lined the kitchen counter. In vain, Jan searched the gathering for Hatch. Margaret had abandoned her and she was on the verge of leaving when Sophie tugged at the hem of her sweater.

"Daddy's coming."

The words warmed Jan's heart. He hadn't forgotten her.

A man close to the counter motioned for Hatch and spoke to him. Hatch shook his head and turned toward Sophie and Jan. Another scowl marred his face as he lowered his head. The other man whistled and when the crowd quietened down, he said, "Lunch is ready. Let's pray."

After the prayer, a chorus of "amens" signaled the folks to form a line. Hatch ushered Jan and Sophie along. He filled two plates and followed Jan to a table.

Margaret bustled over. "Hatch, darling, can I

squeeze in here?" She didn't wait for a reply and chose the seat between Hatch and Sophie.

Jan sat opposite Hatch, not wanting to be close to the pushy beauty. *Stray, indeed.*

A tall man wearing a dark suit stood behind the chair next to Jan, and asked, "May I join you?"

"Of course." Hatch reached across the table and shook hands. "Welcome. I'm KC Hatcher. Is this your first visit here?"

"Yes. Richard Carson. I'm new to the neighborhood." He adjusted his black-rimmed glasses.

The elderly couple Jan had sat beside in the auditorium joined their table. Hatch made introductions and as Jan and Richard were visitors, the couple, Nell and Allen Short, asked them lots of questions. Amid the chatter from the diners and the clatter of dishes, Jan answered with minimal personal information, whereas Richard provided numerous details. Single, recently promoted—hence the move to San Antonio—and an avid sports fan.

Toward the end of the meal, Nell introduced a topic that encouraged Jan to open up. The Shorts had recently visited Paris and praised the Louvre Museum for its collection of paintings by the Old Masters, the Mona Lisa by Leonardo da Vinci being the most famous.

Richard added that he'd been enthralled by many artists, but especially Titian's work, The Madonna of the Rabbit. "The painting includes such a variety of subjects. The scenery and people are depicted with a touch of whimsy."

"I've never been to Paris, but I'd pit the Rijksmuseum in Amsterdam against any other. Talk about being enthralled. I couldn't keep my eyes off The Night Watch by Rembrandt. The way he highlighted certain subjects. Pure genius." Jan folded her arms, confident in her opinion. She turned to glance at Richard, never expecting him to be interested in the Old Masters, too.

And so the banter continued until they'd all finished their dessert. Jan noted Margaret did not contribute to the conversation but frequently cast menacing glances her way.

Hatch's phone buzzed and he checked the screen. "Excuse me, this is important. Margaret, please see to Sophie."

"Of course, my darling." The woman beamed at him and then smirked at Jan.

No big deal. Getting to know Hatch better would have been great, however, Richard entertained her with his quirky sense of humor and obvious interest in her and art in general. Besides, Margaret had a special relationship with Hatch, one Jan was hard-pressed to describe. Love interest or friend?

Nell and Allen excused themselves and left the table, and Sophie wriggled in her seat. "Can I go outside, please, Maggie?"

"Sure, sweetheart." She lifted the child from the

chair and glanced at Jan and Richard. "I hope you return next week." She hurried after Sophie who left the room via a side door.

Jan wiped her mouth and set the napkin on her empty plate. "I'm ready to go outside, too. How about you?"

"Yes, ma'am. That sure was good chili." Richard stood and pulled Jan's chair back for her and then picked up their plates. He deposited them in the trashcan close to the door.

Jan searched in her purse for her car keys and didn't notice the small step from the foyer to the sidewalk. The heel of her boot caught and she almost tumbled, but Richard caught her. "Thanks."

"My pleasure. Here, take my arm. Wouldn't want you to sprain your ankle."

The action wasn't necessary but she'd seem ungrateful if she didn't accept his offer. She rested her hand in the crook of his elbow and had to admit, his thoughtfulness was heartwarming.

"Can I walk you to your car?"

"No, thanks. I want to say goodbye to Hatch."

"I'm so happy I came here today. It was nice to meet you. Do you live nearby?"

Not about to give a stranger her address, she replied, "In the next subdivision."

"Me too. I'm renting a townhouse on River Oak Boulevard."

"That's around the corner from me." She bit her

lip. The words had spilled out of her mouth before she could stop them. She removed her hand from his arm.

"No kidding. I jog through the neighborhood every morning. Well, Miss Sullivan, I hope to see you again. Soon. Will you be here next week?"

"Maybe."

He raised his eyebrows, nodded, and then sauntered to his pickup.

Jan smiled. Richard was an interesting guy. Self-assured, charming, good-looking, with brown eyes, blond hair, and a megawatt smile. And he had a special interest in her as a woman, not an artist. He was the dose of male attention she needed.

She searched the crowd and found Hatch and Margaret talking in an intimate huddle while Sophie examined something in the dry grass. Jan didn't want to eavesdrop, so she stepped backward, waiting to catch his eye. But the pair raised their voices and she couldn't help but overhear the conversation.

"I don't believe you. What's really wrong, Hatch?"

He stuffed his hands into his pockets. "I'm such a hypocrite for welcoming Jan and Richard when I don't want to be here. I claim to counsel people using Christian principles, but I don't feel like a Christian most days. I have such anger and guilt built up in my heart."

Margaret leaned in close and they must have lowered their voices because Jan couldn't hear any more of the conversation.

"Daddy, look what I found." Sophie's statement ended their tête-à-tête.

Hatch turned and noticed Jan. "Oh, don't leave yet." Then to his daughter, he said, "What do you have, honey?"

"It's a funny bug with lots of legs."

"Put it down, Sophie. It's not a friendly insect."

"But Dad, I like it."

Margaret slipped on a pair of sunglasses. "I have to go, Hatch. We will finish this conversation another day." She grabbed his shoulders, looked intensely into his face, then kissed him before striding away.

He shrugged, knelt beside Sophie, and removed the bug from her hand. "It's time for us to go home, honey." Standing, he added, "Jan, I'll walk you to your vehicle."

"Thanks."

"Sorry, I ignored you during lunch."

"That's all right. Richard kept the conversation moving." The recent interaction she'd witnessed between Hatch and Margaret solidified her notion they shared a special relationship. Sophie certainly liked the woman.

"He did. Will you be back next Sunday?"

"I'll think about it, pray about it. Seeking a new church home shouldn't be a frivolous event."

They neared her SUV and he lowered his head. "I hope you decide to return."

She climbed into the vehicle, he closed her door,

then nodded to her and stepped away. Sophie lay her head on his shoulder and smiled at Jan.

While setting her purse on the passenger seat, she glanced to her right. Richard sat in his pickup a few spaces over, talking on his phone. He turned and noticed her. He slipped on his glasses and waved enthusiastically. Jan chuckled at his overzealous gesture, started the engine, and drove out of the parking area.

Still amused by Richard, she clucked her tongue. After meeting Hatch, she'd realized she had emotions that a considerate man had rekindled, and now a second attentive man had added to the reality. She giggled as a positive thought entered her mind. Her heart was open to the possibility of a relationship. At least now she would be more aware if Mr. Right came along. Whereas, previously, he could have danced in front of her and she wouldn't have noticed.

CHAPTER 17

One of the duties Hatch fulfilled at the church was to help Doug Koble, the treasurer, count the contributions. They met in the office and sorted through the money and checks. Hatch was surprised at how many people still used them. Some members preferred online giving, while others used hard currency.

Once the total was entered in the ledger and the funds were locked in the safe, Hatch picked up Sophie who'd been scribbling on his notepad. Thankful she appeared to have overcome her eventful night, especially after he'd cut off the branch that morning, he kissed the top of her head.

Doug, the man who'd asked Hatch to give thanks before the luncheon, walked with him to the front doors. "I don't mean to pry, but you are usually the first to offer a prayer. Is anything wrong?"

Do you have all afternoon? Hatch shrugged. "I have a lot on my mind. Clients' problems and life in general, I guess."

"Let me know if I can help. I'll certainly pray for you."

"Thanks." Hatch walked to his car and drove home with a load of guilt dragging him down. Not even Sophie's singing lifted his gloomy mood. He could have discussed his issues with Doug, but maybe he needed a professional therapist. Sure, he was a successful counselor and he'd helped many people over the years, but he didn't know how to fix his own problem.

After Laura died, he'd coped through the stages of grief, but the guilt only crept into his soul about three years later. She had suffered from postpartum depression, and Hatch had not recognized the symptoms. He hadn't expected her to take care of everything and did his share of household chores, changed diapers, and made sure Laura had time for herself. However, he didn't question when she retreated further and further into a quiet, noncommunicative woman. She'd gone through the motions of being a wife and mother, but she'd lost the sparkle in her eyes and seldom showed any delight in having a beautiful little daughter.

During the preceding year, Hatch had berated himself over and over, and each time, it seemed the burden of remorse grew heavier. He had not read the signs from his own wife! One bright October day, Laura left Sophie with Margaret, drove to a secluded area of their subdivision, and committed suicide by overdosing on over-the-counter cough medicine and pain pills. Now whenever Hatch noticed a woman who exhibited the slightest signs of depression, he felt it was his duty to help her, client or not. His obsession was increasing and infringing on his day-to-day life.

By the time he arrived home, Sophie was asleep. He forced the dark memories from his heart, unbuckled the car seat, and carried her inside where he laid her on her bed. Her shoes removed and the duvet tucked around her and Patches Panda, Hatch went downstairs and made his favorite hot drink, a London Fog. He set the Earl Grey tea bag in the mug and added steamed milk and a touch of honey and vanilla. Sipping the delicious drink, he turned on the TV. Despite his love of football which began when he played in high school and college, he quickly lost interest in the discussion of which teams would win playoff games and who would win the Super Bowl. His thoughts traveled back to the worship service, to lunch, and to Jan.

Leaning back in his recliner, he smiled. He could still recall the jolt to his system when he'd seen Jan sitting next to Nell and Allen Short. She sat in *his* church. He'd gathered from their conversations in the park that she wasn't a stranger to the Bible and today she worshipped where he did.

When she drove out of the parking lot, he'd noticed Richard in his pickup, and a speck of jealousy nudged his heart. He had to admit he didn't like the fact Jan and Richard seemed to have such a good time during lunch. Not that Hatch was sorry Richard had come to church, after all, newcomers were welcome, but he seemed so attuned to Jan. Hatch knew nothing about the Old Masters. In fact, he knew nothing about art and he'd never traveled outside the USA.

He thumped his thigh. *You oaf. Could it be Jan had fun conversing with Richard because you had been too focused on your own problems?* But she had come to Deer Park, a direct result of her reading the details on his card. If she returned next week, he'd have to pay special attention to her.

Football forgotten, Hatch changed clothes and tromped outside to rake leaves, a chore he'd neglected for weeks. Lost in the rhythmic action, he recalled events from the past two years that had made him cynical and suspicious where women were concerned. Ever since Laura's death, he had been pursued by single—and sometimes not so single—women. A successful and independently wealthy man with a young child was fair game and a highly valued catch. He'd been propositioned, cornered, and occasionally bribed. Sometimes the bait was food. A casserole, a cake. Sometimes it was an appeal for help repairing a faucet, or a squeaky door hinge. He'd gradually become aware of the traps but the ploys were tiresome.

Then one day Margaret came to give Sophie a haircut. She had been Laura's best friend, and after her death had helped Hatch in many ways. She took away Laura's clothes and personal items, babysat Sophie, stocked the freezer with meals, showed Hatch how to do the laundry, and in general, kept his feet on the ground through the grief.

During the visit that day, an acquaintance who lived a few streets over arrived with a chicken casserole in hand. Hatch answered the door. When she was halfway through her flimsy excuse for being there, Margaret strolled down the hall and stood beside Hatch, placing her arm around his shoulders. The woman's expression soured immediately. She stammered a reason for suddenly having to leave, handed him the dish, and drove away.

Hatch remembered thinking then that a close association with Margaret had more benefits than accepting her help and enjoying her company. When Ms. Chicken Casserole saw her, she'd retreated faster than a foe facing a Roman Legion. In the ensuing months, Margaret had acted as a buffer for Hatch on more than one occasion.

He placed the last of the leaves in a bag, carried it to the fence, and squinted at the tree where Sophie wanted her swing. Maybe his plan had worked too well.

Omitting his boorish behavior during lunch from the equation and Richard's presence, he wondered if Jan had been as pleased to see him as he was to see her. She certainly didn't give much away, except in the parking lot when Margaret said goodbye to him. Had he glimpsed a fleeting moment of disappointment flash across her face?

His turn to be cynical. Was his interest in Jan genuine or because he sensed she had a deep-seated hurt? He shook his head and returned to the house. Sophie woke a few minutes later. When he picked her up, she curled her arms and legs around him. He cherished the warm, sleepy embrace and sweet smell as he carried her into the living room and sat down.

"Can you make my swing tomorrow, Daddy?" she asked.

"I'll try, honey."

They sat for a while, Sophie probably soaring through the air on her imaginary swing, Hatch wishing he'd introduced Margaret as his good friend, especially when he recalled the guilty twinge when Jan said he had honest eyes. Sophie squirmed out of his lap, ran to the hall closet to her toy box, and returned with crayons and paper. Hatch watched her little fingers manipulate the fat crayons. He folded his arms to keep his love-filled heart contained in his chest. As the most important person in his life, he would do everything in his power to give Sophie a stable, loving home.

With that sentiment in mind, he acknowledged Jan was the first woman he'd met since Laura's passing who'd captured his interest. And yes, he admitted, he needed to know more about her before he could let her into the core of his life—providing she was interested in him. If not, he still wanted to know what secret produced the shadows in her eyes.

He might never be able to let go of his need to help every wounded woman he met.

CHAPTER 18

On the way home, Jan stopped at an electronics store, purchased a smart doorbell, and arranged for its installation. Meandering through her subdivision, she drove past Marybeth's house and noted her car in the driveway. The perfect time to have a chat.

Jan parked in her own driveway and walked to Marybeth's house before her courage took a vacation. She knocked and heard a faint mumble, and then the door opened. Marybeth towered close to six feet, had a medium build, and kept her straight, gray hair short. She had been very attractive in her younger days—as Jan knew from photographs she'd seen. But her sour expression marred the hint of beauty remaining. The expression hardened when she saw Jan.

"What do you want?"

"May I come in, Marybeth?"

She stared her up and down as if trying to find something new to criticize. "I suppose."

Leading the way to her living room, Marybeth sat on the sofa. Jan followed and chose a straight-backed chair. She glanced around wide-eyed. Newspapers lay strewn about. Empty coffee mugs littered the table, and layers of dust covered the usually pristine surfaces. Marybeth's housekeeping skills were slipping.

Jan almost forgot her reasons for visiting, but the scowl on Marybeth's face reminded her.

"I'm waiting." Marybeth propped her feet on the coffee table, a no-no on Jan's previous visits.

Eyes on the big feet, Jan said, "Marybeth, I have something to say and I'd appreciate—" She held up her hand when the older woman opened her mouth. "I'd appreciate you letting me finish." Jan took a deep breath. "First, I want to apologize for my attitude. I know you miss Bryan very much and you blame me for his disappearance. But I did not harm him. Yes, I knew he had doubts about the marriage. So did I." She held up her hand again when Marybeth leaned forward. "Please. I've told you why I believe he's alive, and I'll share that again with you if you'd like."

Marybeth hung her head, lips pursed, silent.

Scooting to the edge of the seat, Jan continued. "We're on the same side. I'm sure sooner or later Bryan will let you know where he is and why he left."

When Marybeth raised her head, tears pooled in her eyes.

Jan held out her hand, but instead of accepting the gesture, Marybeth stood quickly and strode to the window, leaving Jan grasping at thin air.

Marybeth turned, hands clutching at her rumpled sweater, tears streaming down her cheeks. "I listened to your…your nonsense. Now please leave. I have nothing to say to you. I don't care what proof you say you have, it's still all your fault. Now go."

With purse in hand, Jan stood. "I only want to help, and I have another question."

"Get out! I said, get out!"

The menacing figure loomed over her and Jan scurried for the exit. Marybeth slammed the door, and Jan stopped on the sidewalk. She glanced up and down the street, then back at the house. Something was not right with Marybeth. The state of her house reminded Jan she needed to ask Inez to intervene regarding the medication issue. Rats. Jan had no chance to ask if Marybeth knew anything about The Thugs. Should she go back and broach the subject?

A curtain in the living room window twitched and Marybeth glared at her. Not a good idea.

Slinging her purse over her shoulder, Jan headed down the street and around the corner to Inez's house. She rang the doorbell and waited. Knocking brought no response. She didn't know Inez's phone number so searched in her purse for a business card to leave.

A car stopped in the street and Inez struggled out of the dark sedan. The plump woman waved, and the car drove away.

"Hello, dear. What can I do for you?" The exertion of walking up the driveway left her short of breath.

Jan smiled but watched the car slow at the corner. "Sorry to bother you, but I have a favor to ask."

Pulling her keys from her purse, Inez unlocked the door. "Sure, come in, dear."

Jan recaptured the image of the dark sedan and shook her head. There were many such vehicles.

She followed Inez inside.

CHAPTER 19

With a fresh sheet of paper on the slanted board, Jan began painting the last picture for the book. As she swiped blue across the top of the page, squealing brakes and the loud engine of the garbage truck reminded her she hadn't set out her trash. She raced downstairs, opened the garage door, and wheeled the bin to the curb in time for it to be emptied.

The chill in the air seeped through her thin painting smock and she rubbed her arms. A man jogged along the sidewalk and when he reached her neighbor's yard, slowed and walked toward Jan. She recognized the wavy blond hair and glasses. Richard. "Good morning."

Breathing heavily, he set his hands on his hips. "Well, if it isn't Miss Sullivan. How are you?"

"Fine. Would you like a drink of water?"

"No, thanks. I'll wait until I get home. Hey, are you redecorating?" He pointed to her paint-splattered smock.

"I'm painting, but not my house. I'm an artist."

"Nice. No wonder you knew so much about the

Old Masters. What's your forte?"

"A bit of everything. Illustrating children's books, which is what I'm doing now. Landscapes. Portraits."

"No kidding? I need a portrait artist. My parents want one of *moi*." He patted his chest. "They already have my sister's."

Jan studied his face. He seemed sincere. And she had no pressing business once the last pictures were approved by Vince. "I could do it for you."

"That's perfect. Tell you what. I'll go home, shower, and change then can I come back to discuss the details?"

"Sure."

"Great. See you in thirty minutes." He jogged off down the street.

Business was business. Rather than inviting clients into her home, she rented studio space at the gallery for her portrait work. Considering the recent events, she wouldn't make an exception this time.

She returned to her studio and worked on the painting. Halfway through, the doorbell rang. She slipped on a jacket and after checking the peephole, met with Richard on the front porch.

Settled in one of the rocking chairs, he asked, "How do you go about this process?"

"Instead of making a client sit in the same position for hours on end, I take several photos. Standing, sitting, headshots, different poses. Then I sketch an outline on the canvas and with the client's approval, I begin painting. I only require the client to sit for me during the final stage to make sure I have the face perfect.”

“That makes sense. What paint do you usually use?”

“Oil, and that means you won’t be able to take the portrait right away. The drying time will depend on how many layers of paint I use. If you prefer, I can use acrylics.” She handed him a brochure detailing the sizes available and her price list.

“Oil will be great. I see here you have a studio downtown. Is that where I’ll have to go?”

“For the final sitting, yes.”

He ran his fingers through his blond curls. “But you’re painting pictures for the book here.”

“Right, but not portraits.”

“Can you take the photos here?”

“Sure.”

“Good. I started a new job and work from home. Your house is more convenient, but I understand.”

“My number’s on the brochure.”

“I have a major commitment today. Can I come back tomorrow wearing a suit—which my parents requested?”

“Call before you come to make sure I’m home. I have several paintings to deliver to the gallery.”

“Thanks. My parents are celebrating their fiftieth anniversary next month. How long will the portrait take?”

"It depends on the size."

He studied the brochure. "I think sixteen-by-twenty-inches will be great."

"And do you want head and shoulders only, from the waist up, or full body?"

"So many choices. How about from the waist up? How long will it take?"

"Probably a week, if I can concentrate on it. I only work a few hours at a time."

Richard stood and stuffed the brochure into his pocket. "The timing is perfect. My folks will be surprised. I'm sure they expect me to have a large photograph made, which I would have done if I hadn't met you."

"I require half the cost upfront. See you tomorrow."

"Okay." He descended the steps and then jogged along the sidewalk.

Jan returned to her studio and sighed. She'd seen a different side of Richard. On Sunday, he'd been entertaining. Today, he was all business. And she liked the fact he wanted to please his parents.

When the last painting was complete, Jan set it on the counter to dry, then changed her clothes and secured the River Walk paintings and three landscapes in the SUV. She locked the car door, opened the garage, and then drove out, not about to make it easy for The Thugs to get to her.

During the drive downtown, Jan reflected on her

time at Deer Park Church. She'd felt at peace right away and closer to God. She knew worship was not for her benefit, but to honor the Father, and if attending the church helped her change her attitude, then it was worthwhile. In time, she would get more involved. Ward Reeves, the preacher, had listed several opportunities in his introductory remarks.

At the gallery, Francisco removed the paintings from her vehicle while Jan spoke with Pat.

"Last week we discussed the possibility of doing a selection of wildflower pictures."

"Right. I can begin on them this week, but I also have a portrait in the works. If he pays me tomorrow, I'll need to use your studio."

"It's available."

"Wonderful. Bye." Jan had reached the front door when Pat caught up with her.

"Wait, *mija*. I almost forgot. Remember you painted three landscapes for the new bank branch in Boerne. Nathan Yeats, the manager, will mail you an invitation to attend the opening."

"That's exciting. Thanks."

When Jan arrived home, she noticed the gate to her backyard was ajar. Once safe in the house, she dumped her jacket and purse on the kitchen counter and peeked through the blinds covering the French doors to her patio. No one there and nothing seemed amiss. She hurried outside and closed the gate. Redd Carlson, a gardener employed by many residents in the neighborhood wouldn't have visited as the winter-brown lawn needed no attention. The wind could have blown open the gate but…

Pinpricks of unease poked Jan's neck.

She set the alarm and then noticed Hatch's business card next to a bowl of fruit on the counter. His headshot in the corner displayed his dimpled smile. Jan recalled the heated conversation she'd overheard in the parking lot. Margaret hinted Hatch might need therapy, and he allowed her to reprimand him. He did fit the image of Jan's fantasy fellow, but since he and Margaret were an item, she packed away her romantic notions. Besides, he seemed troubled, and Jan didn't need to add to the load of problems she had with The Thugs.

Back to business. The paintings for the book were dry and she needed to send them to Vince ASAP. She didn't have a high-powered scanner for large items, but an office supply store close by did. The process didn't take long. The cover had been painted on an eleven-by-fifteen-inch page, while the content pictures were on seven-by-ten-inch pages.

She texted Vince, and when she reached her driveway, glanced at the gate. It was closed. How would The Thugs make contact? Jan imagined various scenarios, each one worse than the last. Leaning against her locked kitchen door and with the alarm set, she rolled her eyes and said, "Quit scaring yourself."

Painting would ease her mind. She worked late

into the night on the Texas wildflower pictures Pat had requested, listening to Rock and R&B hits on her iPod. Jan chose to paint the flowers in acrylics, on twelve-by-sixteen-inch canvases that could be displayed individually or as companion pieces.

Relying on sketches and photographs from the previous spring, she began with the familiar bluebonnet, orange lantana, and pink evening primrose. Then she completed the more unexpected—the gold Cowpen daisy with feather-edged petals, clusters of purple verbena, the overlapping, swirling petals of the white rain lily, and finally, the delicate lilac basketflower with thread-like petals.

Ready for bed at two in the morning, she rubbed her stiff neck and shoulder muscles. The concentrated effort had exhausted her supply of energy. She slid between the covers, closed her eyes, and let out a long sigh.

A racing engine blasted the night air outside her house.

Alert and on edge, she sat up. Tiptoeing across the shadowy room to the window, she peeked through the blinds. Half expecting to see a dark sedan, relief flooded through her at the sight of a light-colored pickup that roared off down the street.

Sucking in air, Jan crept back to bed, but her thudding heart kept sleep away for a long time.

CHAPTER 20

Initial greetings over, Hatch studied Tracy while she removed her coat and settled in an armchair across from him. Dressed in a dark pantsuit and with her curly hair neatly framing her face, she bore little resemblance to the woman who'd visited him ten days ago. This Tracy entered the office without hesitation, hands calm and a half smile on her face. She crossed her legs, flicked a piece of fluff off her knee, and focused wide, dry eyes on him. When she'd rescheduled their appointment, he'd surmised she wouldn't show. But here she sat, as if she'd come to discuss the weather.

He usually began all but the first visit with a question. *What have you done this past week to improve your situation?* But he'd barely opened her file when she leaned toward him.

"Mr. Hatcher, I've made up my mind. I want to contact the shelter. Can we call them right now?"

Floored but relieved at her words, he set the file on his desk and nodded. "Certainly. I'll support you any way I can in this decision."

As he lifted the receiver of his landline phone, the buzzer on his outer office door signaled someone had entered. For new clients, a sign above a file basket instructed them to complete a questionnaire. He wasn't expecting anyone, but sometimes people walked in off the street. Another sign on his inner office door indicated when his current session would end. Hatch hoped the person would wait.

Next thing he knew, the door swung open and Wendall stormed in. Hatch dropped the receiver.

Tracy melted into the chair, confidence replaced by fear. Her hands flew to her face as she brought her knees to her chest.

"I knew you were sneaking around on me." Wendall's deep voice didn't match his beanpole body. He stepped toward Tracy, deep lines etched in his anger-flushed face. "Followed you, slut. Get up." The man grabbed a handful of his wife's hair.

On guard, Hatch stood and stepped toward Wendall and Tracy. Hands in a *stop* position, he focused on the man's dark eyes. "Mr. Taggart, please sit down. Let's discuss this situation."

"Discuss what? That you've been messin' with my wife?" Spittle droplets and whiffs of alcohol accompanied his words.

Swiping at his face, Hatch balanced his weight and flexed his knees. Mid-morning and the man was well on his way to intoxication. Bad sign. "Tracy, get up and leave."

"She's not going anywhere." Wendall tugged so hard on her hair that he pulled some out by the roots.

Tracy yelled and placed her hands over her temple. "You brute." She glared at him, stood, and took a few steps toward the door.

"Oh, no, you don't." Wendall pushed her backward then leaped at Hatch like a starving locust on harvest day.

Unprepared for the sudden move, Hatch lost his balance, knocked over the side table, and landed on the floor with Wendall's arms and legs wrapped around his body. Fending off blows, he latched onto the man's shoulders and turned, pinning him to the ground. He outweighed Wendall by at least fifty pounds, but his wiriness kept him in the fray—a kick to the kidneys, a punch to the jaw. After dodging a right hook, Hatch grabbed the fist, twisted his arm, and spun Wendall around, face down. It took all his strength to keep the man on the floor, but finally, he prevailed by sitting on the back of his knees and holding Wendall's fists behind his back.

Panting, he glanced at Tracy. "Call the police."

Face blanched and drawn, she shuddered.

"Tracy, please, get up and call the police."

Wendall struggled and mumbled. Hatch tightened his grip and bent close to the man. "You've had your say." More colorful words lingered on his tongue, but he held them back. "I need your help, Tracy."

That awakened her spirit. She stood, and hugging the far wall, made her way to the desk. Her eyes never left her prone husband. In a quavering voice, she described the situation to the 9-1-1 operator, then sank into Hatch's desk chair.

"Good job, Tracy. Thank you. The police will be here soon. You're safe." Hatch repeated reassuring phrases to her while maintaining his hold on Wendall.

By the time the squad car arrived, Hatch's hands were almost numb. He flexed his fingers as the officer slipped her handcuffs around Wendall's wrists. The other officer gathered the facts and then escorted him outside.

Adrenaline still surging through his muscles, Hatch paced to the window and back. *That was close.* He'd never been attacked before. Pumping a fist into his palm, he glanced at Tracy now back in the armchair. She seemed to have shrunk two sizes. Shoulders slumped, face pale, panic-tinged eyes, she looked like a whipped animal.

Hatch settled in his chair and took a deep breath. "You can go home today, Tracy. Your husband will be charged with assault and battery. Should keep him in jail for five to eight days. You have that much time to decide what to do."

As she raised her head, he saw a glimmer of hope in her eyes.

"You can come for another visit and we'll call the shelter." Her eyes darted back and forth, but he kept talking. "Or you can call."

With a quivering sigh, Tracy stood. "Thank you, Mr. Hatcher. I'll pack some things and take my children to the shelter tomorrow." She headed to the door and turned. "I…I'm so sorry." Glancing at the smashed side table, she shrugged. "I'm sorry."

Hatch escorted her out to her car, not his custom, but anxiety still cloaked her every move. She drove away without a backward glance. He kicked at a piece of gravel and rubbed his jaw. He'd have a bruise there soon. Would it show before he took Sophie to the birthday party at Canfield Park?

CHAPTER 21

Wearing a navy-blue suit which enhanced his blond curls, Richard walked with Jan through the gate to her backyard. She'd hesitated about where to take his photos and decided to stick to her code and not invite him inside.

"I'll take some shots with you wearing your glasses and some without."

He shook his head. "Only with glasses, please. I've worn them since I was eight and I can't abide contacts. My folks might not recognize me without them." He gave Jan a thumbs-up sign.

The session in the garden didn't take long. Richard's dazzling smile and athletic build guaranteed every pose to be a winner. Even the black-and-white shots were great.

She showed him the pictures and he'd made her laugh by giving a catwalk description to each photo.

"Here is our model, Richard, wearing the latest Italian suit. Or maybe it's made on Mars. See, it has a red sheen." Or, "Look at his amazing physique. He must be able to bench-press at least…ten pounds.”

After a bout of laughter, he began to cough. And cough until his eyes watered.

“Hey, come inside for a drink of water.”

He nodded and followed her into the kitchen. The niggling cough continued until he'd emptied the glass. “Wow.” He cleared his throat. “I'm okay now. Allergies. Only since I moved to Texas.”

“Yeah. Mountain cedar pollen is bad this year and there are numerous trees in the field across the road.”

“No wonder. It doesn't help that I forgot my meds this morning.”

“Where did you live previously?”

“Arizona. I'm not allergic to anything there.” His phone buzzed and he checked the screen. “Excuse me while I reply to this text.” Thumbs rapidly tapping the screen, he nodded toward the front door. “I need to go home.”

She walked with him down the hall. “I'll work up a sketch and have you come by to approve it before I begin painting. And remember, I require half the cost upfront.”

“Thanks. I remember.” He opened the door and turned to give her a dazzling smile.

Shadows darkened the doorway. Harold and Tom barged in, knocking Richard to the floor.

Jan gasped. Hesitated. Reached for her cell phone, but Harold grabbed her wrist in a vise-grip.

Tom slung a backpack over one shoulder and said

to Richard, "Get up."

Richard stood and lunged toward Tom, but he stepped aside and Richard hit out at thin air. Then, he punched Tom, but again the man dodged, and this time grabbed his arm and twisted it behind his back.

The men, both wearing gloves, forced Jan and Richard to the kitchen. Harold gave Richard his glasses which had flown off during the fracas, produced a coil of rope from the backpack, and tied Richard to a chair. "That should keep you out of our way for a while. If you yell out, I'll gag you."

"Why are you doing this?" Jan asked, but she knew the answer. Their presence didn't immediately alarm her. They weren't the usual home invaders since they wanted specific items.

"You are going to help us search for the items Bryan left with you." Harold shoved her forward. "We won't hurt you as long as you behave yourself. Put your phone on the counter."

Tom drew Richard's phone from his pocket and placed it beside Jan's. "Since we're in the kitchen, I'll begin here." He opened a cabinet and then pointed to the wooden block holding a set of knives on the counter. "Oh, lookie here." Selecting a carving knife, he waved it in Richard's direction but glared at Jan. "If you don't do as you are told, I'll mark up his handsome face. The scars will impress the ladies."

During the past two weeks, The Thug's threats had only been verbal, but the possibility of physical harm hovered over her and she swallowed against the mass in her throat.

Harold tied Jan's wrists in front of her and led her toward the stairs. "We'll search the bedrooms. Up you go."

"Fine. Let's begin in my art studio." She was thankful Harold accompanied her. He seemed more level-headed than Tom.

"Okay."

"Please be careful in here. I have original paintings that are precious to me. Bryan never spent much time in here. I assure you, there's nothing of his in my house."

"Pardon me if I don't believe you." Harold opened cabinets and moved objects around. Rummaged through the drawers and the closet.

"It would help if I knew what you're looking for. Are these items big or small?

"Did Bryan live with you?" He banged a closet door closed.

"No. He had an apartment."

"What happened to all his belongings?"

"His mother sold his furniture and took his personal things home. Maybe she has what you're looking for."

"Nope." Harold pushed Jan out of the studio. "Next room. Our informant was certain Bryan left something with you. What about his laptop?"

"He must have taken it." While Harold dumped Jan's shoes out of their boxes, she sank onto her bed.

"You're making a big mess."

"Tough. What makes you think Bryan took his laptop?"

She huffed out a sigh. Recalling events from the day he left made her heart ache. Bryan hadn't answered his phone and didn't respond to emails or texts. He didn't stop by after work as he usually did. Marybeth hadn't heard from him and neither had his friend Eduardo. Jan had gone to Bryan's apartment to see if he had fallen, or worse. The place was unusually messy as if he'd been in a hurry to leave, but no signs of a struggle.

"After a few days of no contact, I reported him missing and went with the cops to his apartment. I paid more attention to absent items and noticed his laptop was gone right away. I checked his closet and concluded he'd taken clothes, a suitcase, and everything from his file cabinet. And his car was not in his parking spot. The police determined no foul play had taken place and there was nothing they could do." Jan didn't add that Bryan had also cleaned out his bank account.

"And he hasn't contacted you?"

"No." Jan gritted her teeth. "Obviously, he doesn't want anyone to know where he is."

Harold grunted and led Jan to the spare bedroom. He searched everywhere and then took her downstairs. They walked past the hall closet. The door was ajar, all the hanging clothes had been moved to one end of the rod, and lids had been removed from plastic tubs on the top shelf.

Jan stopped. That was the closet where Bryan kept his coat, and where she'd stowed his CDs and DVDs. Since he had a key to her house, he could have hidden something before he left and then retrieved it at the same time he took his few belongings months later.

"Quit stalling. Get into the kitchen."

"But I have something to tell you."

"It can wait." Harold pulled Tom to a corner of the room where they conversed quietly.

Jan stood beside Richard and asked in a low voice, "Are you all right?"

He nodded. "Except for a bruised ego. Sorry, I couldn't stop them. How about you?"

"Angry at the intrusion."

"I imagine."

Tom approached Jan. "Sit."

She complied, and he tied her torso and legs to the chair. "Don't do anything silly like scream for help or I'll gag you. I still have the knife and won't hesitate to use it."

Harold loomed over her. "Okay, what do you have to tell me."

She told them about Bryan's visit. "He might have taken the item you're looking for then. I seldom use that closet and wouldn't have noticed if he'd hidden something small in there."

"You just now remembered?"

"Well, how was I to know he might have had

something else in there?"

"We have no way of knowing so we'll continue our search." Harold nodded to Tom and they stomped up the stairs. Soon she heard the access door to the attic open. The hinges squealed like squabbling mice.

"Hey, I have some information." Richard looked toward the stairs. "Quickly, before they return. I overheard Tom on the phone. They're looking for a ledger—"

"As in a large book?"

"Yes. He said Bryan took one from his office."

"How would he know that?" Jan frowned. "And why would Bryan have a physical ledger? He worked on computers all day and often complained of eye fatigue. This doesn't make sense."

Richard shrugged. "What job did he have?"

Shaking her head, Jan leaned back. "Bryan was an accountant at Woodward Insurance Company. If he hid anything here he would have done it the day before or the day he disappeared. He couldn't keep a secret and he would have blabbed. Besides, a ledger for a large company would be…large. I'd have noticed something so out of place." The rope made her wrists itch and she tried unsuccessfully to loosen a knot with her teeth. "I'm surprised they didn't say they were looking for a bag full of cash."

"Why?"

"News reports at the time of his disappearance indicated he'd embezzled a lot of money from the company."

Chuckling, Richard shook his head. "If that were the case, Miss Sullivan, he wouldn't have taken physical cash. He would have transferred funds from their accounts to his own."

Jan's turn to chuckle. "Of course. Silly me." She sobered. Did he close his bank account because it included illicit money? No, he wouldn't have been so naïve to use the same back she did. No, no. For all his faults, she didn't believe he'd steal anything.

To change the subject she asked, "Did Tom go into the garage?"

"Yeah."

"They certainly have made a thorough search. It will take me hours to put everything back in place."

"I can help."

"Thanks, but I'll manage."

Harold ran down the stairs, followed by Tom.

"Did you find what you were looking for?" Jan smirked at the brothers.

"Not yet." Moxie sauntered past Jan, and Harold picked her up. "Don't call the cops. We'll know if you do. Remember what happened to your sister and your cat."

Jan squirmed. Blood heated by anger and fear raced through her veins. "Put her down."

Harold set the cat on the floor, patted Jan on the head, and grabbed the backpack.

With that reminder, the men left her house.

On the verge of tears, Jan clenched her teeth. She would not cry. Instead, she stared at the rope around her wrists and twisted her fists back and forth, back and forth. The knots weren't tight, and she managed to free her hands. She untied the other ropes around her and then helped Richard.

"Thanks." He rubbed his wrists. "When Tom wasn't looking my way, I did try to loosen the knots." He picked up his phone and shoved it into his pocket. "My offer stands. I can help you tidy up."

"I'll do it."

"Okay. I'm sorry you had to endure this. Have these guys bothered you before? How do your cat and Delaney figure in their plan?"

"I'd rather not talk about it right now." Too much to share with a virtual stranger.

"I understand, but will you call the police?"

She shook her head.

"Why not?" He studied her face. "Ahh, Harold's threats."

Moxie meowed and rubbed against Jan's legs. She picked her up and held her close. Tom or Harold could have easily taken her.

"She's a good-looking cat." Richard stroked Moxie's soft fur. "I don't feel right leaving you alone after this…intrusion. How about we have a cup of coffee? Or I can cancel my next appointment and take you out for lunch."

Both suggestions sounded like positive ways to put

her mind at ease, but she decided to stick with sketching or painting, which always proved relaxing. "Thanks for the kind offer, but I'll decline."

"A raincheck?"

"Maybe." He'd tried to be gallant and his concern for her seemed sincere. "Okay. Call me." Jan walked toward the front door.

Richard opened it, peered left and right, and said, "No intruders."

His grin helped alleviate some of Jan's frustration over the chilling episode. Back to reality. "I'll let you know when the sketch is ready."

"You have my number?"

"I added it to my contacts when you called to schedule today's appointment."

"Okay. Take care."

Jan closed the door behind Richard and set the alarm. She collected her phone and was about to call Teagan, but hesitated. Her sister's involvement would certainly put Delaney's life at risk. Taking into account Harold's hint that they'd know if Jan called the police, maybe she could talk to Sergeant Voss face-to-face in an unofficial capacity, in a neutral setting. Since the men wore gloves, there'd be no fingerprints. She didn't know what vehicle they drove. Voss already had their physical descriptions, but now she was sure they worked for Woodward Insurance or had some connection to the company.

She dialed Voss's number but had to leave a

message. "Guess who visited me? Please call so we can arrange a meeting away from the station and my home."

CHAPTER 22

Chicken salad sandwich and water bottle stowed in the backpack, Jan drove to Canfield Park. Sitting in the sunshine and doodling would clear her mind. She needed to surround herself with everyday normality. The task of tidying up her house could wait. As she strolled through the playground, hordes of children scampered about. Two tables decorated with plastic cloths and birthday balloons dominated the picnic area pavilion.

She chose a bench at the opposite end and opened her backpack. Pad set on her lapboard and pencil poised, she viewed the celebration, speculating which child had turned a year older. Her hand moved over the paper, lead marks scratching here and there, capturing the cacophony of running kids, balloons, and birthday hats. For the most part, the activity suppressed memories of The Thugs in her house, but occasionally, an icy shiver scurried across her shoulders.

Holding the completed picture at arm's length, she viewed it from different angles, then quickly erased the features of one of the boys. Too realistic. She altered his mouth and hairline and surveyed the scene. Maybe she should leave. Her tension had eased and she needed to provide a sketch for Richard. She would not let the incident interrupt her work.

A little girl squealed behind her and she turned. Sophie held a blue balloon and ran with a group of kids. Hatch might be here, too. Considering his relationship with Margaret, she didn't want to see him. She picked up her backpack ready to escape, but felt a tap on her shoulder.

"Jan?"

She froze.

Stepping around the bench, Hatch smiled. "Hi. I thought it was you."

"Hatch, hey." She glanced at him for a second, then fumbled with her sketch pad and backpack.

He cleared his throat. "We're here for Isaac's birthday party."

"Birthday. Right."

A little depression formed as he stubbed the toe of his boot into the pea gravel. "Are you sketching for another book?" He pointed to the pad poking out of her backpack.

"No, no. Doodling. Enjoying the sunshine." Yanking it out, she smoothed the page.

"Some doodle. It looks like a party."

"Can I see? Can I see?" Sophie squeezed between Hatch's leg and the bench, eyes scanning the page.

"Where's me?"

Chuckling, Jan flipped to a clean page. "I'll draw you right now." With eyes flitting from the child's face to the page and fingers flying across the parchment, Jan soon produced a simple portrait of Sophie.

She angled the pad so Sophie could see. "There you are."

"That *is* me." Her blue eyes grew wide. "Daddy, look."

"Yes, honey. It's almost like a photograph." Smiling at Jan, he asked, "May I have it?"

"Sure." Jan signed and dated the page, tore it out, and handed it to him.

"Thanks." Hatch studied the picture. "This is great. I'll frame it." He prodded his toe in the gravel again. "Would you like to join us?"

Jerking her gaze to the partygoers, she shook her head. "No, thank you. I must leave. I needed a break and came here to…relax. Painting or sketching always soothes my soul."

Carefully holding the portrait, he nodded. "That's a meaningful sentiment which I'm sure has helped you many times."

Jan frowned. Hatch had on his counselor hat.

"Do you get all your supplies from Supreme Art World?"

Intrigued by his quick change of subject, she said, "Yes. Why?"

"Last week, I saw you leave the store."

He remembered seeing her. "I only needed one tube of paint that day."

"And I visited the DIY store to help a…friend choose flooring."

Hatch seemed to have a lot of female friends. "Were you successful?"

"Yep. Eva was so pleased with my help that she insisted we go on a date." He rubbed a red mark on his chin.

Another friend? "I have to leave."

Bending down, he picked up a pencil. "This must be yours."

"Thanks." She shoved it into her backpack.

"Speaking of dates—"

"Hatch, Terry, kids, time to cut the cake." The voice of Birthday Boy's mother interrupted their conversation.

"Come, Daddy." Tugging at Hatch's hand, Sophie tried to backstep.

He allowed the child to pull him away but said over his shoulder, "I hope to see you next Sunday."

With Margaret by your side? Jan sighed.

Parents and kids sang to the birthday boy and he blew out the candles. Jan took the singing as her cue to leave. She zipped up her jacket and strolled to the parking lot. A black sedan pulled into the lot and appeared to be waiting for her spot. She slipped into her car and buckled the seat belt.

The black car moved behind her, blocking her

exit, and stopped. She started the engine and waited. The black car didn't budge.

Exasperated, Jan mumbled, turned off the ignition, and climbed out.

Now she recognized the vehicle.

Harold glared at her from the driver's seat and opened the window. "Is there a problem, Ms. Sullivan?"

Standing by her open door, she swallowed hard. "You know very well there is. Move so I can back out, please."

"Although we didn't find what we were looking for at your house this morning, we still believe Bryan left something with you."

Tom leaned across Harold and said, "Our informant told Ed—"

"He assured us Bryan took…a book and hid it at your house."

The anger returned and gnawed at Jan's gut, and sweat popped on her brow. At least he admitted what they were searching for. "Why are you looking for it a year after he left?"

"No comment," Harold said through gritted teeth.

"I don't know where he is. I don't know about anything he left at my house. Your threats have gone far enough. Move your vehicle before I call the police."

Tom climbed out of the passenger door and rounded the vehicle. He stood so close to Jan, she could smell mozzarella cheese and pepperoni on his breath.

"Do you have a storage unit? Did Bryan have one?"

She backstepped. "No, and no."

He pounded the hood of Jan's SUV with his fist. "Then we might have to dig up your garden."

"You wouldn't dare."

Grabbing her arm, Tom scowled. "Now look here, don't get smart with me."

"Leave me alone." Jan struggled to pull free.

"What's going on here? Jan, do you need help?" Hatch's voice behind her acted like a siren.

Tom let go, bent, and whispered, "Tell your boyfriend to watch out." He backed away, hurried around the car, and yelled, "Is Bryan worth it?" Then he jumped in the vehicle as Harold sped off.

Jan rubbed her arm and leaned against her car.

"Who was that guy? Did he hurt you?"

Fear now raised its head and joined her anger. "No. I'm okay, thank you."

"Do you want me to call the police or take you home?"

"I'm fine."

"Are you sure? I could get Sophie and leave with you."

Jan exaggerated a smile. "Really, I'm fine. I'm sure it was all a misunderstanding and I don't want to interrupt the party."

"The guy was bald, right?"

"Both men are. Why?"

"Last Saturday night, Sophie woke me and said she

saw a bald man outside her window. Which is strange since we live in a two-story house."

"There are lots of bald men around." Jan frowned as Tom's last words scampered through her mind. "It doesn't hurt to be careful."

"I know. Sophie might have had a bad dream, but I installed a security system yesterday, anyway."

"Good. Thanks again for your offer of help. Go back and enjoy the party." She slid into her car and drove away. Seeing Hatch and Sophie again had lifted her spirits, but the appearance of her foes hurled her back into the pit of anger and trepidation.

However, besides reporting the home invasion to Sergeant Voss when she met with him later that morning, she had two additional items to add to her list. Tom's threat regarding Hatch—whom she assumed he meant by her "boyfriend"—and she'd memorized three digits from their license plate.

CHAPTER 23

With the list displayed on his phone, Hatch pushed the cart up and down the grocery store aisles. The last time he shopped, he forgot Sophie's juice, and she'd pouted all through supper. He didn't want a repeat performance and added two cartons to the cart.

In the produce department, a woman had reached for an apple and knocked one to the floor. He bent to retrieve it seconds before she did the same.

Glancing at her, he stood and smiled. "Jan. What a surprise."

She straightened her sweatshirt and swiped a strand of hair out of her eyes. "Hatch."

They stared at each other, then Hatch held the apple out to her. "This yours? Seems I make a habit of picking things up for you."

"I already have one. I don't buy too many at a time." She brushed at the paint flecks on her shirt.

Hatch eyed his phone. "I have a list."

"Good. Lists are good. I should make one myself."

Slipping his phone into his shirt pocket, he kept his

eyes on her face. "Any repercussions from those men at the park yesterday?"

She shook her head.

"Good." She held his gaze, but he wished she'd feel comfortable enough to share her troubles with him. "It looks like you've been painting."

"I'm always working on a project."

"Um, last time we met—" A subtle alarm beeped from his watch. "Sorry." He tapped it. "Time to pick up Sophie at daycare. That's my reminder. I need reminders like alarms and lists."

"Did she enjoy the birthday party?"

"She did, thank you." He placed the apple back on the display and turned his cart. "Have those men bother you again?"

"No."

"Good. I'm sorry, time for me to go. Bye."

At the quick checkout, he gave himself a mental thump. He should have stayed a few minutes longer and asked her out. How else could he discover what caused the frequent shadow to cloud her eyes?

Ten minutes later, Hatch buckled Sophie's car seat. "Have fun today, honey?"

"Yeah. Isaac brought his computer game. It was a birthday present."

"Computer game. Great. I'm making your favorite for supper."

"Can I swing first?"

The rope swing had been a big hit. He'd set it up a

few days ago and every opportunity she got, Sophie asked to be pushed on it. "Okay, honey."

"Yippy, yippy, yippy. Are we having hotdogs for supper?"

"No. Tacos." Those were her favorites last week.

"Did you 'member juice today?"

With a chuckle, Hatch snapped his seat belt. "Yes, Sophie. Today I remembered my list. I bought juice."

He pulled out of the parking lot and glanced in the rearview mirror. She flipped through pages of a book and hummed.

Juice. Her world would survive. She had juice.

Hatch groaned. Juice. Could his conversation with Jan have been any more stilted? *I have a list today.* He couldn't have been more tongue-tied if he'd had a mouthful of rubber bands.

The encounter with her at the park had sent his pulse racing. When he'd seen the man grab her, visions of Wendall's fists and Tracy's bruises battered his mind and he'd sprinted like an Olympian to the parking lot. *Not again. Not another person I care about.*

Waiting at a red light, Hatch repeated his thought out loud, "Humph. Person I care about?"

Admitting his interest in Jan took him by surprise. Since Laura's death, he'd compartmentalized his life so much he hadn't left room for romance. But something about Jan's handling of the situation in the park troubled him. She said she didn't know the two men or why they attacked her, but she hadn't been completely honest with him. He could tell by the way she averted her eyes.

Hatch drove through the intersection and scratched his head. Why did it matter if Jan kept something from him? *It matters because she matters.* He'd never met anyone like her before. In the grocery store, she'd looked so down-to-earth and cute in her paint-speckled sweats and messy hair. It said volumes about her confidence to appear in public without makeup and not perfectly dressed. Her image still sent his senses into orbit. In his experience, he found most women who obsessed over their appearance to be shallow. Even though Jan had pulled at her shirt and fiddled with her hair, he'd noticed a spark in her eyes. Almost a spark of defiance. As if she said, "This is who I am, like it or leave it."

"I like it."

"What do you like?" Sophie asked.

"I'm talking to myself, honey."

Entering his garage, he added to the list of qualities he needed to know about Jan. How would she and Sophie get along? Only one way to find out. After supper, he'd call and ask her out. Her acceptance would indicate she had an interest in him, and based on his counseling experience, he knew the questions to ask to get her to share her ideas and desires about her future.

He supervised Sophie on her swing for fifteen minutes and then prepared the tacos as quickly as he could, but Sophie had a dozen stories to share as they ate. He shoved aside his desire to phone Jan and gave Sophie his full attention during the meal and later as he read to her and listened to her prayers. Only then, did he make the call.

Rocking back and forth in his office chair, he held the phone to his ear. It rang and rang. His throat tightened. He swallowed. Another two rings. The call went to voicemail. He hung up. What message could he leave?

Sweat popped on his upper lip. He rubbed it away, whiskers prickling his fingers. Was he being too hasty to ask her out so soon? But he wanted to get to know her better and…

He dialed again, and this time she picked up after four rings. "Hello, Jan." His voice croaked. He cleared his throat. "Hatch here."

A long sigh wafted over the airwaves. "Hi."

"Am I calling at a bad time?"

"No." She took a deep breath. "I was in the attic."

No need to ask why. "I want to apologize for acting like a doofus in the store this afternoon."

Finally, she chuckled and her tone lightened. "We're even then because I *looked* like a doofus."

"Never." Although her hair had poked out in various directions, nothing could have hidden her high cheekbones and full lips.

"You need your eyes checked." A noise in the background indicated she moved about. "I have a lot of work to do. I'll talk to you later."

Her words acted like a dousing of cold water. He stood and paced. "Hold on, please. I have something to ask. It's short notice, but would you like to go out with me on Saturday evening? I have a couple of things I'd like to discuss." Slumping back into his chair, he waited, breathing on hold. He should have omitted that last sentence.

One second, two. Three, four. What if she said no?

"Okay. What time?"

Jumping up, Hatch marched to the window. "Um, how about seven?" Was that too early or too late?

"Seven is fine. Where should we meet?"

"I'll pick you up."

"Thanks, but I'd rather drive myself."

"Sure." Interesting. "There's a new Mediterranean restaurant on Copper Stone Drive."

"I know where it is. See you there."

He hung up and punched the air. "Woohoo." If the evening was a success, that is, if he could convey his interest in her and ask some soul-searching questions, he'd explain his relationship with Margaret. And he'd tell Margaret about his interest in Jan.

Streetlight glinting off a car caught his eye and he glanced out the window. A black sedan had parked across his driveway with a person at the wheel. As he made his way to the front door, his gut twisted. Was that the same car he'd seen at the park with Jan? He opened the door. The car's motor purred. Stepping closer, he spied two men in the front seat. Sure they were the same guys, he bent to get a better look, but the car sped away.

Hurrying inside, he dialed Garret's number. The call went straight to voicemail. He texted his urgent need to talk and sat at his desk. While he waited for Garret's call, he had plenty of work to occupy his time and turned on his computer. Hours passed before insurance billing codes and clients' names meshed in front of his eyes. After catching the fourth error he'd made, Hatch closed the accounting program.

He climbed the stairs and his cell phone rang. Garret, returning his call.

"Do you have any info for me?" He worked his jaw side to side. The bruised area began to ache.

"Sorry, it's taken me so long to get back to you. I'm in the middle of a missing person case. There was nothing on the surveillance tapes from the parking lot to help us. But two men have been nosing around your lady friend for a while."

Lady friend. Hatch liked the sound of that. "Do you know their names? I saw their car outside my house tonight."

"No, I don't but I did get a nibble on a year-old news story. Hang on." Garret's muffled voice rose in alarm. "Urgent business. I'll be in touch."

Hatch stared at the phone. Call ended. Garret gave him no names, but he did provide one lead.

Returning to his office, he logged onto the San Antonio Express-News website. They had archived stories going back more than a decade. But without a definite topic, his search came up empty. That is, he found nothing to help him determine why the two men harassed Jan. He did read several articles about her work. An art show along the River Walk; her landscapes purchased for a hotel lobby; and her acceptance as a permanent artist in *La Casa de Colores*. House of colors. Great name for an art gallery.

The only story of any interest from a year ago featured a man who'd embezzled a fortune from his company and disappeared. His name was Bryan Buchanan. Bryan? One of the men at the park mentioned that name. Did he have a connection to Jan? Saturday's date now took on a different hue.

CHAPTER 24

The sketch for Richard's portrait took Jan longer than expected. She couldn't decide on a pose. Formal Richard standing with his arms by his sides, a serious expression on his face. Or casual Richard, smiling, tie removed, and hands on his hips.

She settled for a mixture of both. A casual pose, smiling, but with his tie knotted. Once she made the decision, the bones of the portrait took shape quickly. For a background, she would add splashes of color, representing his effervescent personality.

Standing back from the canvas, she studied the sketch. "Looking good, Janyth. Time for a break." She rolled her tight shoulders and went downstairs to make a mug of hot tea. The microwave dinged and she grabbed the mug and almost dropped it when the doorbell chimed. The newly installed smart doorbell system had cameras aimed at the front and back doors. It sent an alert to her phone and a video of whoever rang the doorbell. However, it was useless since Jan had left her phone in the studio. Approaching the door with unease nipping at her heels, she peeked through the peephole. Inez Nash. Whew.

Jan opened the door. "Hi, Inez."

"I took a chance you'd be home. Do you have a minute to discuss Marybeth?"

"Yeah, come in."

"No, I can't stay long. I asked Marybeth about her meds."

Joining her on the porch, Jan asked, "What did she say?"

"She's very secretive about them and it took me a while to gain her confidence. Anyway, she takes two different medications. I promised I wouldn't tell anyone what they are or what they're for—"

"I don't need to know the specifics. Is she taking them?"

Irene nodded. "She assured me she takes them regularly, and it didn't look like she needed refills."

"Then I don't know what could be causing her behavior change." Jan shrugged. "Thanks for trying."

"I'll see what else I can find out. We're becoming good friends. I must hurry. Bye." She held onto the railing while descending the three steps and then waddled down the driveway.

Back in the kitchen, Jan sipped her tea. She was concerned about Marybeth but there wasn't much more she could do.

Later that afternoon, another doorbell chime interrupted Jan's wildflower painting. She squealed when she recognized Teagan on her phone and ran downstairs.

"Hey, sis. It's so good to see you." She drew her eldest sister into a hug.

"Okay, okay. You don't have to squeeze the breath out of me." Teagan's deep voice matched her physique. Her sweats did a good job of hiding her well-toned body. Keeping fit was her passion. At five-foot-nine, a marksman, and proficient in martial arts, few fellow police officers could match her record or best her in training exercises.

"Are you—"

"Between assignments. I'm parched. Make me a cup of coffee, please."

"Sure." Jan linked arms with her and walked to the kitchen. "Have a seat. Are you hungry?"

"No, thanks." Teagan sat and stretched her long legs under the table. "I just returned to my condo and need to unpack. Then, I want to sleep uninterpreted for days. Endless nights of surveillance have deprived me of my shuteye."

"Did Sergeant Voss contact you? Is that why you're here?" As Jan set a pod in the coffeemaker, she surveyed the room and smiled. She was so glad she'd cleaned up the mess The Thugs had made.

"Yeah, but also to visit my baby sister."

Jan threw a dish towel at her. "As you can see, I'm fine. And I'm not a baby."

"I know, but you'll always be my little sis."

Teagan patted her neat chignon. "How do you like my new hairstyle?"

"Since when do put your hair up?"

"It was part of my undercover image. But when I get home, all the hairpins will come out. Quit stalling. Tell me about your home invasion."

"That's a bit…strong." Jan placed the mug of coffee in front of Teagan and sat. She related all that had occurred two days ago and included the note left on Delaney's phone when she'd been tied up.

"You're sure those men didn't hurt you?"

"Yes. I promise. They made me angry more than anything." Jan tapped the table. "Something else bothers me. Harold said he'd know if I called the cops. That's why I asked Sergeant Voss to meet me away from my house."

"Pass me your phone. Did either man have access to your cell?" Teagan swiped the screen several times.

"Yes. Harold made me leave it on the counter before I went upstairs with him. Why?"

Teagan swiped the screen again and said, "Aha. They installed spyware on your phone. They can track your calls, texts, and other transactions. I will remove what I found, but take it to your provider so they can do a deep search for other malware."

Knots twisted in Jan's gut. She held her stomach and groaned. "They must be desperate."

"I agree. Voss visited Woodward Insurance, but the clerk in Human Resources told him there were no employees who matched Harold and Tom's descriptions, and a license plate search came up empty."

"That's interesting because they knew too much about Bryan not to have some connection to the company."

Teagan set down her mug. "The men didn't find what they were looking for but they could come back."

"Why? Unless they want to rip up the floors, or as Tom said, dig up the garden."

"Please consider moving in with me for a while."

Jan leaned back and rocked the chair on two legs. "Thanks, but I'll be fine here. I'm extra vigilant when I go out and I have the smart doorbell with cameras at the front and back doors."

"I noticed."

"These intruders must have super tech skills. They found out where Delaney was house-and-pet-sitting, they know about a guy I met at the park, and—"

"Wait. What guy?"

Jan described her meetings with Hatch and her visit to Deer Park Church. An image of his chiseled face popped into her mind, but as quickly, Margaret's svelte figure joined him. Jan shook her head.

"Tell me more. Why'd you leave Hillside? This Hatch chap—your tone takes on a special quality when you talk about him. Does he attend Deer Park?"

"Slow down with the interrogation." Jan scooted back from the table.

"I'm concerned about you. You haven't always been a good judge of character."

"Don't throw my past at me, please. I've matured and won't rush into a relationship again. I learned my lesson with Bryan."

Teagan giggled. "I'm sorry, sis. I'm tired and am not thinking straight. I'm sure this Hatch guy is terrific."

"He might be, but there's a beautiful woman at Deer Park Church named Margaret and…I think they're a couple."

"Would it bother you if they were a couple?"

"Maybe. I like him, he seems interested in my work, but—"

"Why don't you ask him about Margaret?"

"I will. He's taking me out Saturday evening."

"That's a good sign, isn't it?"

"I won't get my hopes up. He has offered me counseling several times. This date might be his way of having a captive audience so he can *fix* me."

"If that transpires, at least you'll know where you stand. Anyway, keep me posted. Delaney said you're texting or calling each other every day. While I'm in town, please include me in the loop."

"Have you seen her?"

"No. She's in class. When you text her today, tell her I'll stop by the house tomorrow. After I've caught up on my beauty sleep."

"You need plenty—"

Teagan scowled at her, stood, and pretended to bop her on the head. "Can I convince you to move in with me?" She yawned. "Sorry, bab…Janyth, my dear sister. I must go home."

Jan shook her head. "I have commissioned landscapes for the gallery and I'm working on a portrait. I need all my painting supplies close at hand. Thanks again, but I'm staying here." She followed Teagan to the door.

"Take care."

Jan hugged her again. "Will do. Go home and rest."

"I'll wait on the porch until I hear you lock the door."

"Okay." Jan closed and locked the door and set the alarm for good measure. She leaned against the wall. Her conversation with Teagan has stirred up emotions about Hatch. And Richard. She knew little about the latter, but he expressed an interest in her and as far as she knew, didn't have another woman in his orbit. Besides, she liked him.

And Hatch? She knew more about him, but she'd been hurt enough times to be skeptical. Saturday's date, or whatever it was, would answer many of her questions.

CHAPTER 25

The alert on Jan's phone displayed an image of Richard standing on her porch. She invited him in and walked to the kitchen.

"I hope you suffered no ill side effects from what happened the last time I visited." He shoved his hands into his pockets and surveyed the kitchen.

"I'm fine, and I feel much safer with the smart doorbell system."

"Too bad you didn't have it a few days ago."

Jan set the canvas on a table-top easel. "I'm kind of glad Harold and Tom searched my house. I hope they'll leave me alone, now."

Folding his arms, Richard studied the sketch. "That's pretty good."

"Only pretty good?"

"Bad choice of words. It's excellent. I recognize myself."

"Who did you think you'd see?"

He withdrew an envelope from his jacket pocket and set it on the table. "I'm digging myself in deeper every time I say something. So, since I'm already sinking, I'll throw out more words. Have lunch with me after church on Sunday."

A meal with Hatch Saturday evening, and lunch with Richard the next day? That was one way to get to know them better, and what did she have to lose? "Okay. Thanks." She opened the envelope and eyed the cash inside. Interesting. Most clients paid by card. "I need to take several paintings to the gallery this morning. I can begin your portrait today. Do you want a receipt now or when I complete the painting?"

"Later will be fine. I checked your website. You're a talented young lady."

The praise never got old. "I enjoy my vocation."

"I'm looking forward to seeing the finished product, and to lunch on Sunday. See you then." He turned and headed to the front door.

This time she had her phone in her pocket. No alert meant no one was on her porch. She hurried behind him.

Richard took the three porch steps in one stride and climbed into his truck. He waved and said, "Your hair looks cute like that."

Like what? Jan touched her messy bun, smiled, and stepped inside. Richard's presence always lifted her spirits. She hummed as she gathered the wildflower paintings, the sketch of Richard, and a few supplies.

Once set up in the gallery studio downtown, Jan added a small amount of liquin to a blob of cobalt blue and titanium white on her palette and stirred the colors together. She painted across the pre-primed canvas, avoiding the face as much as possible. One of the joys of using oils was she could paint over any color later. She'd printed several of Richard's photos and studied one of the black-and-white shots with a good balance of light and shadows on his face.

By one o'clock, she'd added skin tones to his face and outlined his suit. When doing portraits, Jan had to stop after a few hours of concentrated effort. Despite sitting to avoid back strain, her neck and shoulder muscles were tight. She headed home for a late lunch.

The familiar figure of Marybeth ambled along the sidewalk past Oscar's house. Jan's positive mood remained even as the woman lingered on the sidewalk. Jan opened the garage door and drove in all the while keeping her eye on the rearview mirror. Marybeth now stood in the middle of the driveway.

Even though their last meeting had been unpleasant, Jan tried to add a friendly note to her words. "Hi, Marybeth. Can I help you?"

"No," Marybeth said in flat, heavy tones. "Done any digging yet?"

"If you mean the tree in my backyard, then the answer is no, and I don't intend to." *How dare she?* Jan trudged toward the woman, trying to keep her anger corralled.

"We thought not." Marybeth tugged at her sleeves.

"We?"

"Harold, Tom, and me. They were here, um, yesterday."

"Did you invite them?"

"No. They came to visit me. I showed them your house and the tree."

"You did what? You went into my backyard?" By this time Jan reached Marybeth and because of the driveway's slope, stared the taller woman in the eyes.

"No. Look." Marybeth tramped onto the lawn and pointed beyond the fence. "The tree's visible from here. I didn't go in your yard."

With her hands thrown on her hips, Jan glanced over her shoulder. "Are you sure? Because my gate—"

"Are you calling me a liar? I told you *I* didn't go into your backyard." Marybeth marched back to face her. "I'm not a liar, but you are. I still say you killed my boy."

All control snapped. Jan's words spewed out cold and hard. "Get off my property. Don't ever come here uninvited again and that includes your friends."

Marybeth stormed off.

Disturbed by her rage, Jan carried her backpack inside and set the alarm. The Thugs in the backyard? Why?

~*~*~

Saturday chores were put on hold while Jan searched her closet for something to wear that evening. Many items did not fit well due to her weight loss, but that couldn't take all the credit—or blame. She was also extra critical. Finally, chose a pair of black jeans, a rose-pink silk blouse, a coordinating sweater, and black boots.

Delaney had invited her for a light lunch so the three sisters could catch up. Jan had time to begin vacuuming, not her favorite. How could a house get so dirty with only one woman and a cat as residents? When she finished, she checked her cell phone. A missed call. From Hatch. She dialed his number, hoping he wouldn't cancel their plans.

"Sorry, I missed your call. Vacuuming."

"Want to come over and help me? I hate vacuuming."

"No, thanks. I hate it too." She hesitated, not wanting to know why he called, but anxious to find out.

"Anything wrong?" His voice held a note of concern. "Can you still come tonight?"

"Yes."

"Great. I have a babysitter for the whole evening. What would you like to do after we eat? That is if you want to extend the date."

Put on the spot, Jan shrugged. She still didn't consider it a date and hadn't thought beyond the meal. "How about a visit to the River Walk? I haven't been there for ages."

"Good idea. Sophie's calling me. How about I pick you up? No sense taking two cars."

"Okay." Jan rattled off her address and hung up.

She didn't bother to change out of her sweats for

the visit with her sisters. What a treat, to spend an afternoon with them. Seldom were all three Sullivan girls available at the same time. They had become closer as young adults, especially after Jan injured her back at a homecoming football game. The bleachers collapsed and she ended up at the bottom of a pile of teenagers, metal, and wood. A section of her spine was damaged and she had to have spinal fusion surgery again.

They certainly weren't close when they were kids. As the youngest child with medical issues, her parents had paid her a lot of attention which her sisters resented. They thought Jan had been spoiled. It wasn't until they were old enough to realize the seriousness and extent of the surgeries she'd endured, that they realized they'd been unfair and changed their attitudes.

With all that drama behind them, Jan only received love, support, and encouragement from her sisters. She parked in the driveway and entered the large house, smiling and full of gratitude for her siblings.

During the get-together, Teagan shared what details she could of her undercover assignments, Delany reported Mrs. Ingram's attitude toward her had warmed, and Jan's contribution included her upcoming meal with Hatch.

"Ooh, your first date. You must tell us all about it." Delaney nibbled on a dip-covered chip.

"I will, but I'll only call it a date if he doesn't offer to solve my issues and if he explains Margaret's place in his life." To switch the focus off herself, Jan asked Teagan, "What happened to the detective you were dating?"

"The relationship fizzled out. He couldn't deal with my days and weeks of being incommunicado." Teagan hiked a shoulder. "I've resigned myself to being single. What about your love life, Laney?"

Leaning back in her chair, Delaney chuckled. "We're three peas in a pod. I've given up looking for the right guy but I pray every night that God is preparing the man for me."

Jan hung her head. She hadn't prayed for guidance in regards to Hatch. Or Richard. Later in the afternoon, on the way home, she voiced an earnest plea, "Father, God, help me to be open to hear Your voice, to be patient, and to strive each day to be worthy of Your Grace."

Chores completed, she stood on her back patio and wrapped her hands around a mug of hot chocolate. The morning clouds had blown away, the late afternoon sun shone, but a chill hung in the air. Bare flower beds, winter-brown grass, and the leafless tree glared at Jan. Unbidden thoughts of Marybeth came to mind. Why would she think Bryan had been buried under that tree? Would this nightmare ever be over? Jan gulped down the last of her drink and scurried back inside.

Ready way too early, Jan paced in her den. Looked in the mirror. Should she wear her hair loose, or tied at her nape with a black ribbon? The ribbon won out.

Hatch arrived on time. When Jan opened the door she stared at him as if she'd never seen him before. Maybe because he was picking her up as if this were their first real date. All joking aside, it did look like he'd taken time to dress for the evening. Navy slacks and sweater, with a pale blue shirt. Hair combed back, waves smoothed out. She'd never noticed how his blue eyes twinkled, and his dimple accentuated his slightly crooked smile.

"Hope I pass inspection?"

"I'm sorry." A flush threatened to betray her. She turned her back on him hoping he wouldn't notice as she closed the door.

"That color top suits you."

"Thanks."

"Do you want to put on your coat?"

"I'll carry it for now."

The restaurant wasn't far away. They had no time to address serious topics during the ride.

Pleasant instrumental music and murals depicting scenes of Grecian islands enhanced the atmosphere, and the naan flatbread dipped in seasoned olive oil kept Jan and Hatch occupied until their meals were served. She ordered moussaka, and he gave the chicken shawarma plate a try.

At first, their conversation was stilted, and then Jan asked Hatch about his counseling practice. If he'd invited her out only to offer advice, she wanted to give him the opportunity.

In between bites, he gave her his work history. "My parents wanted me to continue their real estate business, but when I declined, they supported my career choice. After I earned my LPC, I worked at various not-for-profit agencies but often ran into problems when my, um." He paused, then added, "When my Christian values determined a course of action that conflicted with their policies. Using part of the inheritance I received from my grandfather, I opened my own practice where I can help people and not violate my beliefs." He frowned, set down his fork, and folded his arms.

Jan was sure he had more to add, but he switched topics and asked about her career.

"I've always been interested in painting." She decided not to disclose all the details of her surgeries. "I had medical issues as a kid, so my folks provided activities to occupy my time when I couldn't engage in regular play. By middle school, my artwork caught the attention of a teacher and we kept in touch. I received my degree from Texas State, and that teacher was instrumental in getting my first children's book illustrator contract. The commissioned portraits and landscapes followed."

"I admire your talent. It's so broad. The only thing I can paint is a wall." Hatch took a swallow of iced tea. "But I have been wondering about Sophie. She loves painting, drawing, and coloring, and I think she has a good eye for color. Is it too early to see a budding artist in her?"

Jan hiked a shoulder and raised her eyebrows. "I don't know much about child development, but I suppose letting her experiment freely with various media would help cultivate her interest and creativity. Have you asked her daycare teacher?" What was she getting herself into?

"Yes, and she does see more maturity in Sophie's work than some other children her age but said it's too early to tell."

"I'd be happy to look at her pictures if you'd like. Again, I'm no child expert but maybe I can encourage her interest." *How am I supposed to do that?*

"That'd be great. I told her about you being the person who drew *Mr. Caterpillar* and she didn't believe me."

Jan chuckled to hide her unease. She knew Hatch had a daughter, but she hadn't thought far enough ahead to realize if they began dating she would need to get to know Sophie, too. Was she ready for that? She had limited experience with children since few of her married friends had kids yet and neither did her sisters.

The waiter came by and they declined dessert but ordered mugs of cappuccino.

Hatch sipped his drink. "This is good, but I prefer a London Fog."

"A what?"

"My college roommate introduced me to it. Earl grey teabag, steamed milk, add a touch of vanilla and honey."

"Sounds…interesting. Where can I order it?"

"Some fancy coffee shops advertise it, but mine is better. I'll make it for you one day. I hope."

While they consumed their coffee, Jan kept waiting for Hatch to address his hesitation in describing his counseling practice, but instead, he focused on Sophie.

"My little girl is the center of my life. After Laura died, I was in shock. My parents lived in San Antonio at the time. They moved in and took care of Sophie and me for a few weeks."

"You've done a wonderful job with her." That much she could see.

"Thanks. She's a character all right, but I couldn't have done it on my own."

"Where do your parents live now?"

"They retired to Kerrville a year ago. But they're visiting this weekend—babysitting Sophie tonight." He wiggled his eyebrows up and down. "I can stay out as late as I want."

They laughed, and then he sobered and sighed. "Seriously, since Laura's death, I've seldom left Sophie with a babysitter at night."

Jan placed her hand over his on the table. "It must have been hard."

The corners of his mouth twitched upward. "We got through it." He glanced at their hands. "Now, how about you? How come a beautiful, talented woman like you is…single?"

She removed her hand and picked up her mug.

"Oops, did I make a *faux pas*?"

"You did, but I'll forgive you. I'm single because…because the right guy hasn't come along." She stared at the white linen tablecloth. "At least, I thought he'd come, but he didn't stay." She glanced up. Hatch's expression changed from casual interest to concern. Friend to counselor?

Choosing her words carefully, she added, "Long story, but the gist is, I was engaged. Bryan got cold feet and left without a word to me or his mother, and I'm forging ahead with my life." She omitted all the gory details about his disappearance and Marybeth's accusations.

"Any chance he'll return? Do you want him to come back?"

Without giving his questions time to germinate, she shook her head. "No. His decision to leave was the best for both of us."

"I sense there's more to the story." This time, he held her hand.

"There is, but that's all I want to say right now. Thanks for understanding."

While gently squeezing her fingers, he gazed deep into her eyes. "Remember when you're ready to talk, I'll be here to listen."

Hatch's offer interrupted the intimate moment. She pulled her hand away, picked up her mug, and drained it. She didn't need a counselor. She wanted to get to know the man. And to find out Margaret's place in his life.

"It's a positive sign that you're moving forward, but in my experience, people need guidance to work through such a traumatic event. The shadows I see in your eyes at times tell me you still have issues to deal with. That all is not right in your world. I can help you."

It was Jan's turn to lean back and fold her arms. The nerve of the guy. "I agree I have issues, but, Mr. Counselor, so do you."

"Excuse me?"

"I overheard you and Margaret arguing at church last Sunday. Sounded to me like you need therapy." Jan couldn't believe she'd uttered those words. She tilted her head. "I'm sorry—"

"You're right." He shrugged. "I've already had a couple of sessions with a colleague I trust."

Hatch's admission sat well with her, but she was still irritated with him and frowned.

"I suppose suggesting we have dessert at the River Walk is out of the question."

"You are correct. Thank you for the meal, but please, take me home."

He signaled the waiter who brought the bill.

While he paid at the counter, Jan slipped on her coat. Despite their last conversation, she had to know. She stepped outside and shoved her hands into her pockets. *Now or never.* "Hatch, this question has been on my mind. Who is Margaret?"

He paused as if searching for the right words. "She's a—"

A loud voice from the parking lot interrupted, "Hey. I'm talking to you."

Before Jan could turn to see who spoke, a man charged at her. Hatch pushed her aside. She stumbled into a nearby vehicle. The sudden movements clashed with her rigid spine.

Straightening, she grimaced.

CHAPTER 26

Without thinking, Hatch blocked Wendall's advance, receiving the weight of his body in his gut. Sucking in air, he tried to grab the man's flaying arms, but they were like a malnourished octopus, waving in every direction.

Off balance, Hatch dropped to the ground and Wendall rolled off. He popped up like a weed and headed for Jan again. She'd landed against the hood of a pickup and stared at them, wide-eyed.

"No, you don't, Wendall. Your fight's not with her. Come after me."

Wendall pivoted and dropped his fist. "You took my woman, so now I'm gonna take yours." As quick as a bullet, he grabbed a handful of Jan's hair. "Come any closer and I'll pull it out." For emphasis, he pulled her head backward until she winced.

"Wendall, let her go." For the first time, Hatch took in their surroundings. Cars were everywhere but not one person in sight. He felt in his pocket for his phone.

"Don't even think about it." Wendall slid a knife from his pocket and held it to Jan's neck.

She choked on a breath.

"Okay. You have my attention. What do you want?"

With a smug smirk, Wendall backstepped toward an alley between the stores. "Tell this woman of yours what you did to my wife."

Hands held out with palms up, Hatch followed. "We talked."

"Yeah, right. What did you talk about?" Eyes on Jan, he hissed, "Tell her what you and my wife talked about."

By now they were in the alley. Light from the storefront glinted off the knife blade.

Even in this situation, to discuss the meetings he'd had with Tracy would break confidentiality, but he had to say something. "We discussed a variety of topics." Jan's wan face, lined with anxiety, filled his vision.

Wendall ran the knife along her jawline and back down to her throat.

Enough. Hatch took another step closer. "Wendall, let her go. You and I can duke it out. She's not involved."

This time Wendall angled the knife and the point pierced Jan's skin. Drops of blood stained her pink sweater. "Back off and tell me where Tracy is. You know she took my kids." Flexing his fingers on the hilt, he growled, "I don't want to do this, but you made me.

Where's my wife? Tell me and I'll let your little friend go."

Anger blinded Hatch. Air rushed into his lungs as he gritted his teeth. He held Jan's gaze. Moving as subtly as he could, he nodded his head back once, looked at Wendall then touched his nose. Had Jan gotten the message?

She blinked.

Shoulders relaxed, feet hip-wide, he arched his brows.

With a sudden jerk, Jan reared back and smashed her head into Wendall's nose.

He grunted and relaxed his grip enough for Jan to slide sideways. Hatch sprang forward. Surprised by the assault, Wendall dropped the knife. As he bent to grab it, Hatch dove and reached it at the same time. He and Wendall rolled in the dirt and trash like two feeding hogs. With both their hands on the hilt, control of the blade switched from Wendall to Hatch, and back again. In the struggle, Hatch secured his opponent in a one-arm headlock. Wendall's breathing slowed and his hold on the knife loosened. As the sole handler of the knife, Hatch wrapped his legs around the other man and held the blade to Wendall's chest, ready to end the battle.

"Hatch, don't do anything foolish."

Although thready, Jan's voice reached his ears. He squinted against the furnace-hot rage that bubbled through him. How dare this jerk threaten Jan? Taking in sharp breaths, Hatch grasped the hilt tighter. One push and it would be over.

"Please, Hatch."

A dribble of sanity diluted the rage. Hatch closed his eyes. How could he have turned into the monster he fought? Throwing the knife to the side, he pushed Wendall off and glanced at Jan.

With one hand on her throat, she cast a relief-filled gaze at him.

Wendall, choking on a lungful of air, struggled to his feet and dashed down the alley.

Sirens punctuated the night air. Why hadn't they sounded a minute earlier?

Placing an arm around her shoulders, Hatch guided Jan back to the parking lot. Too concerned with comforting her, he ignored a splattering of mutters coming from behind a truck until he distinguished a few words.

"Video. YouTube. Viral."

He stepped around the truck.

Two youths aimed their cell phones at him.

One said, "That was awesome. Blood and all."

The other added, "Why'd you let him go?

Hatch turned away. His career disintegrated before his eyes. Once that video went viral, everyone on earth would know he'd messed up.

Until then, Jan needed his help.

CHAPTER 27

The ambulance departed, followed fifteen minutes later by the police cruiser. An officer had collected the knife Wendall used.

Hatch joined Jan in his jeep. The EMTs had treated her neck wound, and he'd explained to the cops how he knew Wendall and what might have prompted the attack. He was not going to press charges as the man was in a heap of trouble already. He should still have been in jail.

Hatch closed the door and turned to Jan. "Are you all right? I think you should have—"

"No, Hatch. No ER visit. Please take me home. The cut is not deep and doesn't require stitches, only those little butterfly bandages. And," she held up a hand to ward off his response. "I recently had a tetanus shot."

"Right, then. Home it is." During the short drive to her house, he gave himself a dozen mental thumps for suggesting counseling. He'd promised himself he wouldn't, but he couldn't help himself because she seemed depressed.

And that's when her attitude changed.

As if his interference wasn't enough, Wendall had erupted on the scene. The results could have been so much worse. To add to the drama, Hatch didn't get to explain the complicated role Margaret played in his life. He was astute enough to know now was not the time, either.

He walked Jan to her porch, and while she unlocked the door, said. "Please let me know if I can do anything. You've had a shock. Make yourself a hot drink and rest." *Again with the advice.*

Jan rolled her eyes. "I appreciate your concern. Goodnight." She entered her house and closed the door.

She might as well have closed the door on any relationship Hatch hoped to encourage. He drove home wishing he could lock his mouth so he wouldn't speak until the ideas had been filtered through his brain. His well-educated brain. He parked in his garage and entered the house through the kitchen.

Mother met him, a worried frown creasing her brow. "You're home early."

"Uh, yes. Long story. What's up?"

"Sophie has a slight fever and she developed the sniffles as soon as you left."

"Where is she?" Hatch followed his mother to the living room where Sophie slept on her grandfather's lap. He placed his hand on her forehead. "She's a little warm. Have you given her anything?"

"No meds, only lots of liquids."

"Thanks, Mom, Dad. I'll take her upstairs and check her temp." He scooped her up and she stirred enough to recognize him.

"Daddy, my head hurts."

"I have a bottle of good-tasting medicine for you." He planted a kiss on top of her head and laid her on her bed. Two months ago, Sophie had a severe cold, accompanied by a headache and a fever. The doctor prescribed over-the-counter medication, and for Hatch to bring her back if her fever rose or her symptoms persisted.

Her present temperature hovered right at 100 degrees. He'd check it throughout the night. With Sophie medicated and in her PJs, he tucked her quilt around her and the panda. She fell asleep right away. He turned on her nightlight and trudged down the stairs. Concern for her well-being added to his disappointing evening

"Is she asleep?"

"Yeah." He reported on Sophie's temp and the medicine he gave her. "I'll check on her frequently."

"We could take turns to sit with her."

"Thanks, Dad, but you two have done enough already."

"Okay, son."

"Come sit and tell us about your date."

"I will, Mother, but first I need to take care of something in my office."

Dad stood and stretched. "I'll make some hot

chocolate.”

Once in his office, Hatch opened an app on his phone, and sure enough, the video of him and Wendell fighting had been posted. However, even when he enlarged the scenes, he couldn't identify his face. Whew. One less problem to worry about.

He stopped at the foot of the stairs, and when he didn't hear Sophie, joined his parents in the living room.

With both hands around her mug, Mother asked, “Tell us more about Jan. Will she be at Deer Park tomorrow? I wish we could stay and meet her.” She paused. “And why did you come home so early?”

Hatch settled in his recliner. “You can meet her another time.” Right before he left for the date, one of the elders from the church in Kerrville had called Dad and asked him to fill in for Preacher Hank who had developed laryngitis. Mother and Dad would make the hour-long trip home in the morning. Hatch huffed out a sigh and was about to describe the evening when Dad slid his arm around Mother’s shoulders.

“Zoe, my dear, give the boy time to answer.”

“He’s avoiding my question, and I think I know why.” She turned to Hatch. “Did you scare her off by offering her advice in dealing with her…issues?”

“Yes.” He set his empty mug on the side table. “Wait. Why did you ask that question?”

“Margaret called while you were gone. When I told her you were out with Jan, she said you might view her as a potential client and mentioned that you were having a hard time coming to grips with Laura's reason for taking her life."

Why would Margaret share those details with his mother? "You don't have to—"

"Hatch, we both admire the way you handled her death and continue to provide a stable and loving home for Sophie. You know that grief doesn't follow a set pattern. Have you discussed your problem with someone?"

"I'm seeing a therapist." He leaned back. "It's been hard to admit I need help."

"That's the first step, right?"

Then Mother gave him *the look* she'd used with him and his sister when they were kids. Piercing stare, head tilted, lips pursed. They knew that whatever question she asked next, she'd tolerate no skimping on the truth.

"Did you offer counseling advice to Jan this evening?"

He nodded, then smiled. "You know me so well."

"You're—"

"If she's worth your time, she'll overlook your zealousness." His father had a knack for curtailing Mother's interrogation which could have lasted all night. "Son, here's my advice. When you are seeking the right woman to spend your life with, you need to do less counseling and more romancing."

Hatch harumphed, then chuckled. "Yes, Dad." If

only he could go back in time and have a reset for the evening with Jan.

Sophie's call for Hatch broke the silence in the room.

He released the recliner's footrest. "I'll check on her and get an early night. Thanks for listening and for the advice. See you in the morning." He kissed his mother's cheek and rubbed his dad's bald head.

Sophie's temperature was unchanged but she was restless. He stayed with her until she fell asleep again.

He left his bedroom door ajar and leaned against the wall. The conversation with his folks planted Jan front and center in his mind. He acknowledged his offer of help added a chill to the evening. But he sensed her question about Margaret was very important to her. He could have answered after Wendell was arrested. On the drive home. At her front door. Why did he evade the issue?

He sat on his bed and set his elbows on his knees. Jan differed from other women he'd met in the past couple of years. She wasn't pushy or insincere and she hadn't tried to weasel her way into his life. He enjoyed her company, and she was easy on the eyes. Very easy. So why his hesitancy?

During the brief time with Jan that evening, he realized Bryan was the man who'd disappeared after embezzling from his company. Whether she knew about the money or not, Hatch concluded Jan still felt guilty and abandoned. She said the romance had ended, but he wasn't sure she had completely let go. Based on his counseling experience, he surmised she would not be able to move forward until the Bryan situation had been fully resolved. And of course, he'd have to find out why the two bald men were harassing her.

Even if Jan accepted his sincere apology and agreed to another date, could he open his heart to the idea of a serious relationship only to have it broken by her running back to Bryan if he returned? Hatch kicked off his shoes. Jan was worth the risk. Besides, if Bryan did return, he'd have to face the consequences of embezzling from his company.

He had to tell Margaret to ease up on her duties as his *protective detail.* She'd get a kick out of the title. Recalling what she'd told his mother, he frowned as he removed his phone from his pocket. He hadn't told Margaret about Jan and her possible depression, but she'd suspected his concern anyway.

When she answered his call, he omitted any niceties. "I believe you had an interesting conversation with Mother."

"I didn't want her to get her hopes up about you and Jan. You know she thinks it's time for you to date again, and I thought your parents needed to know about your emotional issues."

Not your job. "I would have told them later. I didn't want Mother to worry." Hatch had a hard time saying anything critical to Margaret. He couldn't have survived the past three years without her help. But since he had her attention…

"Hey, Margaret. You know how much I appreciate your help, support, and friendship. Mother is right. It is time for me to, um, reconsider my singleness. Does that make sense?"

"Yes, Hatch, my dear." Her soft tone surprised him.

"In the past, you have sort of been my protective detail. You—"

"Your what?"

"You know. Shielding me from the unwanted advances of…women."

Margaret took a couple of seconds to respond. "There were quite a few and I enjoyed the role. There's another one floating around." Now her tone had hardened.

Did she mean Jan? He had to set her straight. "You can ease up on your duties. I really like Jan."

"She's not right for you, darling. Besides, she's dating Richard, the guy who visited Deer Park last week. I can't think why she went out with you tonight. Maybe she needs counseling."

A frozen mass formed in Hatch's chest. Jan and Richard had enjoyed each other's company. If they were dating, why did Jan accept his invitation? He'd have to rethink his strategy. "Sophie's not well. I need to check on her."

"Poor little dear. Do you need anything?"

"No, thanks."

"Hatch, please don't hang up yet. Considering what you said about easing up on my duties, I have to share what's on my heart. When Laura passed away, I helped you for her sake and because she was my dear friend. But the more I was in your company, the more I realized I wanted to be part of your life. Haven't you ever wondered why I never date? Why I'm always available to babysit? It's not a problem because I love Sophie." She paused. "And I love you, Hatch."

He pulled the phone from his ear and stared at it. Her revelation surprised him, and he couldn't find suitable words to respond. "I've got to go." He threw his phone onto the bed.

CHAPTER 28

After the morning service, people filed out of the small auditorium and gathered in groups in the foyer or outside. Jan searched for Richard who had sat beside her, but had to make a phone call before taking her to lunch.

Margaret, dressed in a navy blue suit and a red blouse, hurried toward Jan. "Hatch didn't come today. Sophie's real sick." She placed a well-manicured hand on Jan's forearm. "And he doesn't want any visitors. She needs her rest."

The woman disappeared before Jan could respond. She didn't even know where he lived, and after last night's disastrous…date, she wasn't sure she ever wanted to see him again.

Beaming a luminous smile, Richard joined her. "Are you ready? Do you want to ride with me or take your car?"

"I'll drive. Where are we going?"

"Surprise. Follow me."

Richard stopped at a Brazilian steakhouse a couple

of miles from the church. "Prepare yourself for a culinary delight."

Seated near the fireplace, Jan absorbed the colorful and mysterious atmosphere and devoured the Moqueca, a seafood stew Richard recommended. What a contrast to her evening with Hatch. Richard offered no advice, he didn't probe into her life but treated her as a mentally healthy woman. He shared parts of his childhood that involved moving to interesting locations around the county, including a small oil town in west Texas called Iraan, pronounced Ira-ann, Happy, Texas, and Okay, Oklahoma. They had fun speculating how the towns got their names.

Jan suspected Richard embellished some stories but couldn't remember when she'd enjoyed a meal more. They parted in the parking lot. Despite the great time she'd had, she drove to the grocery store with Sophie on her mind. Teagan had received her next assignment—not undercover this time—and the sisters arranged to spend the afternoon and evening together before she set off the next day. Jan had been elected to take the dessert and purchased a selection of pastries. No doubt Delaney would prepare a variety of finger foods.

Dressed in blue jeans and a sweatshirt, Jan snagged her purse off the kitchen counter. Her phone chimed and she checked the screen. Hatch. Torn between avoiding him at all costs and her concern for Sophie, she let the phone ring and ring. But her concern won and she answered. "Hello, Hatch. How's Sophie?"

"Thanks for taking my call. Sophie's all right. Her fever has subsided, but she's weak and cranky and wants me to hold her. Not that I mind."

"I'm glad. Margaret insinuated her condition was serious."

Silence.

"Hatch?"

"I need to talk about Margaret, but first I must apologize for last night. I'm so sorry I suggested you need therapy. I want you to know it's because I care about you."

"Thanks, but I talk to my sisters or grandmother when I need to vent. So far, they've been great listeners. They offer advice, too, but they don't make me feel like I'm a client."

"Good. You have a built-in support system. Not everyone does, and that's where… Okay, enough from me on the subject." He cleared his throat. "Now I will answer your question about Margaret. She was my wife's best friend. She helped me immensely after Laura's passing and she still does, especially with babysitting. Margaret is a nurse practitioner and works from home. She's part of a healthcare team. Sorry, my thoughts are a jumbled mess. She is just a friend. I am not interested in her romantically." He swallowed. "When next I see you I'll share more about Margaret, but I had to tell you that much today."

Interesting comment. "Thank you for clearing that

up."

Sophie niggled in the background. "I have to go. Wait. How's your neck?"

"Fine, thanks. I took the dressing off this morning. Bye." Jan hung up, Hatch's words flooding her brain. Just a friend. *I wonder if Margaret agrees.*

~*~*~

Jan spent the morning at the art gallery working on Richard's portrait. Satisfied with the background, she concentrated on his torso. She'd paint his hands when she did his face.

By noon, her back complained and her neck and shoulder muscles needed a respite.

Pat knocked and opened the studio door. "I thought you might be ready to pack up for the day."

Rolling her shoulders, Jan said, "Yep. What do you think?"

Pat eyed the painting. "You amaze me how you can capture the weave of the suit material so accurately."

"It requires intense work with a fine brush. That's why I have to quit after a few hours."

"Well, I have good news. I met with a couple last week. They want someone to paint their house, as in a landscape not the inside walls." Pat chuckled. "They live near Kerrville. Can I give them your contact info?"

"Please. Other than supplying you with pictures, I have nothing commissioned after this portrait."

"I'll email you their names and phone numbers.

See you tomorrow."

Jan hummed as she prepared her pallet for the next day. The paint would stay fresh when covered in cling wrap and stored in the freezer. Still humming, she left the gallery and stopped at a furniture store. With another possible commission coming her way, she decided to purchase a new sofa, something that had been on her priority list for a while. The ugly, floral eyesore in her large den had been with her since her college days and needed to be replaced. Based on her previous online research, she knew exactly what she wanted. Delivery of the black leather three-seater was guaranteed for Thursday midday.

Instead of working on Richard's portrait the next day, Jan had to hurry to the new bank branch in Boerne. Nathan Yeats the manager had called her first thing. While transporting her landscapes to the building, two of them were damaged. The web page designer was scheduled to take indoor photographs the following Monday, and Nathan wanted the landscapes front and center.

Repairing minor holes or rips in a canvas wasn't difficult but did require time. Jan parked in the freshly paved lot and lugged her supply case and a used canvas to the bank.

Nathan opened the door for her. "Nice to meet you, Ms. Sullivan."

"Please call me Jan." She surveyed the blank wall in the large entry foyer.

"Yes, that's where the landscapes will be displayed."

"How did they get damaged?"

"Due to construction delays, we had to store furniture and office equipment in our main branch in San Antonio. During the trip here yesterday, some items weren't properly secured in the truck and a file cabinet fell against the paintings. The corner punctured two canvases, one behind the other."

"Let me see them, please."

He escorted her down a hallway to the conference room. "You won't be disturbed in here. Do you need anything?"

Rolling office chairs surrounded the sturdy oval oak table. "Four chairs without wheels, a pitcher of water. Something to protect the table, and plenty of light."

"Light won't be a problem." He raised the window blinds. "I'm curious. Why do you need the chairs?"

"The framed canvases are too heavy for my portable easel. To work on the pictures, I'll balance each one on two chairs that won't roll away."

"I'll be right back."

In the meantime, Jan opened her case and removed the container of gesso, her utility knife, a pad of disposable palette paper, and several tubes of acrylic paint. She examined the paintings lined up against the far wall. The one depicting a typical hill country scene of an old barn and a windmill surrounded by fields of wildflowers, especially bluebonnets had suffered the most damage. A jagged right-angled tear measuring four by three inches sliced through the barn siding and flowers along its base. The most time-consuming task would be matching the paint colors once the patch was in place. The second painting of longhorn cattle in a fenced paddock with a creek meandering beside a rock cabin had a smaller tear, maybe three by two inches, but it left a steer without a head. Repainting his eyes, horns, and speckled hide would be a chore.

Nathan and an employee entered with the four chairs, a painter's drop cloth, and a container of water. Jan asked them to set the paintings on the chairs so they faced the wall.

"Thanks. The tears will be easy to repair. I'll begin today and will complete the touch-up painting tomorrow. However, I'll have to return one day next week to add the sealant. You can hang the paintings in the meantime. I doubt the missing sealant will be evident in the photographs."

"Great. I'm so relieved." Nathan nodded to Jan and closed the door behind him.

She covered part of the table with the drop cloth and organized her materials, and then she sliced the heavy paper dust cover over the rips and exposed the torn canvases. The old canvas provided the patches that she'd measured and cut out. Beginning with the largest piece, she covered it with gesso and set it over the gash, pressing it from both sides of the canvas. Her arms were just long enough to reach. When the patch was in place over the second rip, she turned the pictures until they faced her.

The next step required the removal of the sealant from the affected areas. Paint would not stick to the protective product she'd used on the landscapes. But she'd have to wait until the gesso dried.

After a light lunch in the quaint town of Boerne, Jan returned to the bank. The gesso had dried sufficiently, and she opened the bottle of sealant remover. Using a lint-free cloth, she dabbed the solvent over the scars left by the tears. The sharp smell of the acetone base reminded her of nail polish remover. Satisfied the task had been successful, Jan used a small paintbrush and straightened the threads over each gash. When she added paint, she wanted the surface to be as smooth as possible.

Now came the hardest part of the restoration— matching the paint colors. She opened her paper palette pad and began mixing colors. Adding paint to the affected areas and adjusting colors took her the rest of the afternoon. She stepped back and evaluated her work. The colors of the barn, the steer's horns, and the creek water needed tweaking.

Her aching muscles hinted it was time to quit for the day. She'd complete the job in the morning. To save the paint she already mixed, she scraped each color into small airtight glass jars. Material packed away, she traipsed down the hall and found Nathan behind the teller counter. "I'll return in the morning. When I'm done, you won't be able to locate where the tears were."

"Thank you, Jan. You are one talented lady."

Tied but gratified at being able to salvage the paintings, she reached home in an upbeat mood, however, her garage remote refused to work. Maybe the battery needed to be replaced. She entered the house through the front door, turned off the alarm, and headed to the kitchen. Something was amiss. Silence. No hum from the refrigerator. No time was displayed on the microwave. She flicked the light switch. Nothing. A power cut.

Her first thought raced to The Thugs. They must be responsible. She hadn't heard from them since they accosted her in the park. But before panic mode grabbed a foothold, she called Oscar, her neighbor. His electricity was off, too.

She sank to the cold tiled floor. Moxie sauntered over and rubbed against her legs. Jan stroked her, closed her eyes, and took several deep breaths. Not The Thugs—a neighborhood outage.

The power came back on at eight-thirty, long after Jan had eaten a sandwich and chatted with Delaney about her courses. She was delighted to hear Delaney was enjoying Mrs. Ingram's class.

Hatch had called Jan twice while she worked at the bank. She kept her phone on silent so she could give the repairs her full attention. He left a message asking her to contact him. She figured he wanted to apologize again, however, she did want to check on Sophie.

Surrounded by her pillows on the bed and Moxie on her lap, she stared at her phone. The disastrous date with Hatch had been three days ago and she'd had time to evaluate her response to his persistent offer for counseling. Her reaction had been immature, to say the least. Based on his years of experience he determined she needed guidance, and he was only trying to help her. She ought to be able to ignore his suggestions for therapy and concentrate on the man instead. She liked him, admired his love and concern for Sophie, and for admitting he needed counseling. He believed in the Bible, but she got the impression he was also struggling with spiritual matters. They had that much in common. If only she could believe Margaret was just a friend.

Jan's phone rang and she almost dropped it. Richard.

"Sorry to call so late, Jan, but I'm going out of town for a few days and won't be available to sit for the portrait until next week."

"No problem. I haven't been able to work on it recently. The timing is perfect."

After they talked a few more minutes, Jan ended the call and held the phone to her heart. The date with Richard had been fun, and she would accept another if he asked, but she couldn't pinpoint the reason she would not encourage a relationship with him.

Moxie stretched and jumped off the bed, jarring Jan back to reality. She had a phone call to make. She dialed Hatch's number and he answered right away.

"Hey, Jan. I'm so glad you called."

She began with the obvious question. "How's Sophie?"

"Good. Fever is gone, her appetite is back, and she's full of energy. I'll take her to daycare tomorrow."

"That is good news." Jan didn't want to hear another apology from him, but let him continue.

"I'm still in the doghouse, my self-imposed punishment. I want to reiterate that I'm sorry about derailing our date last Saturday. Even if you don't want to go out with me again, please forgive me for being insensitive."

Not what she expected to hear and she had to alter her strategy. His tone sounded sincere. "Thank you." Regrouping, she added, "I'm sorry I missed your calls. I've been working in Boerne and had my phone switched off. I need to clear my conscience. It's my turn to apologize. I acted like a child on Saturday. I know you want to help me, so let's make a truce. You don't recommend counseling to me, but if you do, I won't walk out on you."

He whistled out a breath. "That sounds great. I can act like a bulldozer at times—"

"Ha. At times? How about every time we meet?"

"Okay. I agree. But I hope we can be friends and converse like two mature adults."

"I'd like that."

"See you Sunday?"

"Yes."

"Sophie's calling me. Got to go."

Jan held the phone to her heart again. She was relieved they had cleared the air, but also a little disappointed he didn't suggest another date. She shook her head. *He's the one who mentioned the word friends.* That was acceptable for the time being.

The next day, Jan arrived at the bank to find Nathan had brought coffee and pastries for everyone in the building. She sipped her drink and examined her repairs. Pleased with the results, she removed the paint from the jars and played with the colors until they matched perfectly. The steer had his head back, and the barn and creek blended in with their surroundings. She viewed the landscapes from various vantage points. Her repairs were not noticeable. "Good work, Janyth." One last job. She turned the canvases over again and applied gesso around the patches, adding another layer of security.

By noon, she'd completed the job, packed up her supplies, and carried them to the foyer.

Nathan called out, "Hey, Jan. Hold up a minute." He entered his office and returned seconds later. "Here's your official invitation for our grand opening."

"Great. I look forward to the event."

"Send me your bill, or I can pay you now."

"I'll email you an invoice."

"Fine. If ever I meet anyone who wants customized paintings, I will recommend you."

"Thank you. I'll let you know when I can return." Jan waved and walked to her car, satisfied with her rescue mission. Pale sunlight streamed through holes in the blanket of clouds, and the daytime temperature was mild for the end of January.

When she arrived home, she made a mug of hot chocolate and opened the sliding door to her back patio. She staggered backward. The mug slid from her fingers, hot liquid splashed onto her shoes and legs. Goosebumps marched over her body, and a chill encircled her heart as if held by frigid fingers. She clutched at the door frame.

"What has she done?"

The tree in her backyard lay broken and exposed. A mound of dirt towered over a huge hole.

CHAPTER 29

Slowly the haze of astonishment lifted and the battering ram in Jan's head eased its pounding. She returned to the kitchen and poured a glass of water, but when she took a sip, she spilled more on herself than she swallowed.

Slumping into a chair, she set down the glass. "What should I do?"

Her chaotic thoughts raced and when the doorbell rang, she almost fell off the chair. Phone. Where was her phone? She checked the screen expecting to see Marybeth on her porch, but it was Redd. Redd Carlson, the neighborhood gardener and handyman.

Jan made it to the door without collapsing. "Hello, Redd."

"Miss Sullivan, you're back. Did I do a good job? Is it deep enough?"

Jan couldn't make any sense of his words. "What are you talking about, Redd? What job?"

"The tree. The hole."

Her tree. She motioned for him to enter, and

plodded to the kitchen. "Come, show me."

He joined her outside. "See. I dug it up like you asked, then made the hole deeper. When will you get the new tree?"

"I still don't know what's going on. I didn't ask you to do this. There's no new tree."

"But, Miss Sullivan, you said—"

"Last summer we discussed how poorly the tree was doing, but I haven't spoken to you for several weeks."

"No, no. The note. You left me a note." A flush camouflaged the freckles on Redd's face and his eyes bugged.

Frowning, Jan turned. "Do you still have the note?"

"Sure. Here it is." He reached into his jacket's inner pocket and pulled out a crumpled piece of notebook paper.

A typed message occupied a few lines.

Redd: The tree in my backyard is not doing well. I want you

to dig it up and then make the hole bigger so we can plant another

tree, a big tree. Can you do this on Wednesday morning, please?

Thank you,

Janyth Sullivan, #2015 Cedar Lane

"Can I keep this?" Jan waved the sheet of paper.

"It's yours, isn't it?"

"No, Redd. I didn't type this. How did you get it?"

"Miss Sullivan, I'm sorry if…" He backed away, removing his cap. Tufts of what red hair he had left on his scalp sprouted out in all directions.

"How did you get it?"

"The bulletin board at the entrance to the subdivision. Where you've left me messages before. The note was there this morning."

"I see. I'm sorry I was abrupt with you. It's not your fault. How were you to know?"

They stared at each other, then at the hole and large pile of dirt.

"What do you want me to do now?" Redd kicked at a clump of soil.

"Can the tree be saved?"

"I don't think so. I cut the roots pretty bad."

"Forget about the tree." She rubbed her temples in an attempt to chase away the threatening headache. "Fill in the hole and dispose of the tree. Come inside when you're done and I'll give you a check."

"But you didn't ask me to do this."

"No matter. I appreciate your hard work the rest of the year. This is not your fault."

"Thank you." He attempted to smooth the wispy hair and set his cap back on his head. "Sorry, again."

Jan picked up the shards of her mug, and poured water on the chocolate mess, sweeping it into the pale lawn. She had a good idea who'd typed the note but wasn't sure what to do with the information.

After Redd left, Jan dialed Delaney's number but had to leave a message. There was probably not much the police could do, but she called Sergeant Voss anyway. Surprised he was in the office, she explained what had happened.

"Do you still have the note?"

"Yes. I can't prove Marybeth typed it." Jan spread it out on the kitchen table. "I have a gut feeling she did since she accused me of burying Bryan under the tree."

"You could turn over the note to the police for fingerprinting, but—"

"It's in a sorry state. Redd had it scrunched up in his pocket and it's smeared with mud."

"If you can prove Marybeth wrote it, you could file charges for destruction of private property."

"I don't want to go that route. Not yet anyway." Staring at the note on the table, Jan shook her head. "When I saw the hole, it scared me. Then anger took over when Redd showed me the note and I realized what had happened. And now I'm sad. Sad that a bitter, old woman can't let go and has to stoop to such levels."

Voss hesitated, then asked, "Why did you call me?"

"To keep you informed, I guess. Sorry—"

"It's all right. Don't do anything foolish."

"I won't, but I am concerned about Marybeth's erratic behavior. On my last visit, the state of her house astounded me. I've never seen it in such a mess."

"Be careful, Jan."

"Okay. Thanks for taking my call."

Jan placed her phone in her pocket. Tapping her fingers on the counter, she stared at the vertical blinds concealing the back door. She'd told Voss she didn't want to take any legal action but she needed to do something. She pushed aside a few slats and glared at the fresh scar in the middle of her dormant lawn. Redd had smoothed the earth, but the tree's removal had marred more than the ground. It had scarred her soul.

Rage bubbled within and her compassion dissolved. She knew what she had to do. No formal complaint to the police department, but a confrontation with the perpetrator.

Throwing on her jacket, she stormed out the front door and marched down the sidewalk to Marybeth's house. The woman opened the door and Jan charged into the living room without saying a word.

"How dare you?"

"Marybeth, hush and sit down."

Probably caught off guard by Jan's forceful tone, the older woman muttered and flopped onto the sofa.

"I know what you did. Don't try to deny it. I know about the note, the tree, and if you don't leave me alone I will file charges against you."

Blood whooshed through her head. Jan had never threatened anyone before. Tension knots twisted in her gut. Her harsh words sounded foreign to her own ears.

Panting for breath, she glared at Marybeth whose pale face registered shock, disbelief, and fear.

The enormity of her actions struck her. Jan stepped back and sank into an armchair.

In a softer voice she said, "Marybeth, it's time to put Bryan's disappearance behind you. And it's time to leave me alone so I can look to the future, too. I'd hate to take legal action. Marybeth, please."

She blinked rapidly. "I don't know what you're talking about. I don't know anything about a note."

Jan frowned at the sincerity of her words. She surveyed the room. Dirty dishes were gone, papers removed, furniture surfaces dusted. Maybe Inez had already sorted out the medication issue. But that didn't resolve the tree problem.

"You may not admit to writing the note, but you did threaten to dig up my tree."

Marybeth nodded. "I'm sorry. I was upset because of the anniversary of Bryan's disappearance, but I didn't touch your tree."

"And you didn't tell Redd Carlson to dig it up?"

She scowled. "Redd? Who's he?"

Jan's sails deflated. If Marybeth didn't know Redd nor arrange for him to dig up her tree, who did? Thoughts warred for supremacy in her mind.

"You said you showed Harold and Tom my tree. Could they have done this?"

Marybeth sighed, pulled her legs up on the sofa, and lay down. "I'm tired. Didn't sleep well. Let yourself out, okay?"

Standing, Jan stared at the prone figure. Marybeth raised one arm and covered her eyes. The yellow sweater had brown stains sprinkled on the cuff. Her pink floral pants clashed with her red shirt. Strange. She usually prided herself on her sense of style. And she kept her shoes on. The rule in her house had always been no shoes on the furniture.

Snores erupted from the sleeping woman. Jan shook her head. No rants and raves from Marybeth today, but something was amiss. Jan closed the door and walked down the driveway, glancing back at the living room window.

"What am I supposed to do?" Make a referral to Adult Protective Services?

She reached her front door and stopped on the steps, a shudder began at her shoulders and ended at her feet. If Marybeth didn't ask for the tree to be removed, the only other logical culprits were Harold and Tom.

CHAPTER 30

While Sophie recuperated at home, Hatch had met with clients using video conferencing, or they'd rescheduled their sessions. Sophie returned to daycare the previous day, and he'd been busy catching up with paperwork. His first session that morning was at ten, and he steeled himself to execute the plan he'd devised late last night. He had to talk to Margaret.

Since the unnerving conversation with her Saturday evening, Hatch had muddled through the days as if stuck in a time warp movie. He saw himself taking care of Sophie, listening to clients and offering advice—which he hoped was sound—and reviewing his friendship with Margaret since Laura's death.

He appreciated her help, even loved her as a sister, but he'd never consciously hinted at a romantic relationship. How could he have been so oblivious to her attentive behavior?

Hatch parked beside her car in the driveway and closed his eyes. During the four days since the conversation with Margaret, he'd had plenty of time to analyze their…relationship. She was a big part of his and Sophie's lives. She was available to babysit, she sat with them at church, and she often came over to cook a meal or invite them to her home. And yet, he had not attributed her actions to love, but more to those of a caring friend. His fault.

At the moment he felt a hundred miles away from God. He'd failed in so many ways, but the need to pray overwhelmed him. He had to ask for help to find resolutions to this complicated situation. Head bowed, he said in an unsteady voice, "Dear Father, please forgive my doubts, my complacency, and my ignorance. Be with me while I talk to Margaret. Amen." He knew he didn't have to pray in fancy phrases, but he longed for the simple sweetness with which Sophie prayed at night.

As he climbed out of the Jeep, Margaret opened her front door. "Hey. What's up? Is Sophie all right?"

"Yes. She's back at daycare. Sorry for not calling first." He entered her house and removed his jacket.

"I haven't started working yet. Want some coffee?"

"Please." The caffeine might provide the jolt he needed. He hung his jacket on the rack and followed her to the kitchen. How often had he sat at the table without a clue that she wanted more than friendship?

Margaret placed a mug in front of him and settled in the chair opposite. "To what do I owe this pleasure?" She smiled at him over the rim of her mug.

Hatch sniffed the nutty aroma emanating from his mug and then took a sip of the hot brew. "Margaret, we must discuss our last phone conversation."

"I agree. You didn't respond the way I thought you would, and this is the first time we've spoken since."

Where to begin? Hatch looked at her. She was beautiful, talented, caring, selfless. But he had no romantic feelings for her at all. He knew what he'd tell a client in the situation, but it was much harder than he'd anticipated. He cleared his throat. "Margaret, first, I've thanked you before, but you must know that I appreciate everything you did for us after Laura passed. And you've continued to help us, me, especially. I'm grateful you are in our lives."

She narrowed her eyes and tilted her head. "I sense a *but* coming."

Nodding, he set his elbows on the table. "There is. *But* I love you as a sister, and I'm sorry if I ever gave you the impression that we could be anything more than friends."

He wasn't sure how she would respond, but he wasn't ready for her frown, scowl, or clenched jaw.

Margaret pushed back her chair, stood, and folded her arms. She glared at him. "What do you mean? All these years I've been involved in your life, in Sophie's life as much or more than if I was your wife. Didn't you ever wonder why?" She paced in the kitchen, then turned, hands on her hips.

Unprepared for her intense reaction, Hatch stood

and reached out to her.

"Don't even think you can pacify me with your counselor jargon." She harumphed. "Some counselor you are. First, you miss the signs Laura must have exhibited at home, and now…me. How could you not tell that I'm in love with you?" She stormed to the front door. "How many clients have you failed? Please leave. This babysitter, cook, and companion is out of business." She slammed the door behind him.

Hatch drove a few blocks then parked along the curb and cut the engine. Margaret's behavior was so unexpected and uncharacteristic. He thought she might cry or plead, but not throw him out.

However, she had a point. What business did he have trying to help people with their problems when he'd made such a mess of his life? Maybe he should go back to cattle ranching. He worked on his grandfather's ranch every summer when in high school and during his university years. The skills he learned then were valuable.

CHAPTER 31

Since Jan had plenty of time to complete Richard's portrait, she didn't stress about missing another day at the gallery. Delaney had called earlier and was coming by to drop off a couple of meals. The homeowners were due home that afternoon, and she cooked all the ingredients she'd purchased while at their house. Jan's mouth watered at the very thought of eating anything prepared by her talented sister.

Delaney arrived just after ten. Jan waited on her porch and helped carry in the disposable containers. "What did you make?" The savory aromas wafted past her nose, too numerous to identify.

"Vegetable lasagna, King Ranch chicken, and a Mediterranean bean salad, which you need to eat today. The other meals can be frozen." Delaney placed two containers on the kitchen counter.

"Thanks. Can you stay for a cup of tea or coffee?"

"No. I have the dogs in the car, homework to complete, and I need to vacuum."

"Another time, then." Jan waved as her sister drove

away. Always mindful of Delaney's fragile psyche, Jan was pleased to note she seemed confident and happy.

The new sofa arrived as Jan chewed the last bite of salad. The delivery guys set it where she indicated, removed the wrappings from the cushions, and carried out the old sofa. The overstuffed black leather, much larger than the old one, coordinated with the other furnishings, but she quickly realized the flow of the room would improve if the sofa faced the other direction. That would necessitate moving the antique armoire. She couldn't move it by herself and thought of Delaney, but she was busy. What about Hatch or Richard? Hmm. With Richard out of town…

She could invite Hatch and Sophie for lunch on Saturday, and maybe she could use the occasion to check out Sophie's artistic ability. Her offer would also remind him of their truce.

When she called Hatch, she had to leave a message. Work on a new hill country landscape occupied her afternoon, and still waiting for Hatch to return her call, she gave herself a manicure. No matter how hard she tried, paint always stained her nails.

He called later that evening. "Hey, Jan? Anything wrong? What can I do for you?"

Assuming she needed help? *Truce, Janyth.* "I have a favor to ask and one to offer." She cleared her throat. "I need some furniture moved, so I want to know if you and Sophie can come to lunch on Saturday, and you can help with the moving, and I can take a look at Sophie's artwork you said you'd show me. Sorry, I'm rambling."

Hatch chuckled. "I think we can manage it. I have a couple of errands, but I could be there at noon. How much furniture are we talking about?"

"An armoire and a sofa."

"Doesn't sound too bad. But Sophie and I expect dessert."

Jan ended the call and entered the kitchen, a smile stretching the corners of her mouth, but it soon turned to a frown. What to prepare? She perused numerous cookbooks and examined her recipe file, but after what seemed like hours of pencil chewing, she chose to serve Delaney's lasagna with a green salad and breadsticks. And ice cream with a homemade chocolate sauce for dessert.

With her weekend plans settled, she returned to the gallery Friday morning and worked on the portrait. She made the background more abstract and concentrated on Richard's shirt and tie. On the way home, she purchased the groceries she needed, and the next morning, vacuumed and dusted, set the table, and made the chocolate sauce.

When the outside camera displayed the arrival of Hatch's vehicle, she stood at the front door waiting for him to ring the doorbell. She didn't want to appear too eager. A minute crawled by. She peeked through the peephole. They weren't on the porch. She opened the door and was surprised to hear Sophie whining.

From the exchange between father and daughter,

Jan surmised Hatch had forgotten to bring Sophie's favorite toy, and she refused to get out of her car seat. The child pouted, arms crossed, and glared at Hatch. He leaned close and Jan couldn't hear the conversation, but it resulted in a successful conclusion. Sophie raised her arms, Hatch picked her up and then reached into the passenger seat for a small, pink backpack and a bouquet.

"I'm sorry you had to witness Sophie's little tantrum. Here." He handed her the flowers. "I hope you like daisies."

"Thanks, I do. Come in."

Sophie didn't look at Jan as Hatch entered the house. She hoped she could win over the child with the planned painting activity.

Hatch walked down the hall to the kitchen and set the backpack on the table. "May I move one of the chairs to—?"

"Ooh, Daddy, put me down. There's a kitty-cat."

"Sophie, first you need to take a four-minute timeout."

Jan held back to allow Hatch to administer the consequences. He scooted a chair to the far corner, set Sophie on it, and removed her coat. Pointing to his watch, he said, "I'll let you know when you can get up. Okay?"

She folded her arms again, but no pout this time. "Yes, Daddy."

Jan opened a cabinet and stood on tip-toe to reach

a vase, but Hatch stepped behind her. "I'll get that for you."

"Thanks." Jan took the vase from him, filled it with water, and arranged the flowers. "They will look good on the table. Excuse me." She left Hatch in the kitchen with Sophie and entered the dining room. The yellow flowers coordinated well with her tan-and-burgundy-stripped tablecloth. Hesitant to interrupt the timeout, she hovered in the hallway.

Hatch saw her, tapped his watch, and mouthed, "One more minute."

She nodded and remained in the hall, counting down the seconds.

"Okay, Sophie, you can get up now." He paused, then added, "What do you need to say?"

"I'm sorry, Daddy. I didn't put Patches in the car. I left her in my bedroom."

He knelt and hugged her. "Thank you for admitting that. I love you, honey."

"Can I play with the cat, now?"

He stood and motioned for Jan to join them. "You have to ask Jan."

The child twisted her little fingers together and approached Jan. "What's your cat's name? Can I play with him, please?"

"Certainly. *Her* name is Moxie." Jan couldn't help but smile at Sophie's eager expression.

Sophie spied the cat in the hall. "Come here, kitty-cat, I mean Moxie. Wait for me."

"She'll be occupied for all day with the cat." Hatched picked up the backpack. "What are we moving today?"

"Come through to the den." Standing at the door, Jan pointed to her new acquisition. "I want to move the sofa over there against that wall which means the armoire has to come this way about ten feet. I've already emptied it."

"That will allow more freedom of movement in a room this size."

"Exactly what I thought."

"Let's get started." He rolled up his sweatshirt sleeves. "I thought maybe you had carpet so I brought these neat things." He pulled a pack of plastic discs from the backpack. "They make moving furniture over the carpet a breeze."

Sophie dashed into the room, following the cat.

"Honey, we're ready to move the furniture now. You must be real still because we don't want you to get hurt. Come and sit over here, please." He indicated a chair away from the action.

"But I want to play with the cat."

"You can find Moxie when we're finished. Now, come here, please."

"Okay." Sophie climbed onto the large armchair and settled among the plush cushions.

Hatch gently placed a disc under each corner of the antique armoire. "This is a beautiful piece of furniture. Is it a family heirloom?"

"No. I bought it a couple of years ago. I like how the bottom half is storage and open shelves are at the top."

"I'll push while you guide it into place." The ancient piece of furniture creaked and shuddered as they inched it across the carpet. Then they tackled the sofa, which was much easier to move.

Meanwhile, Sophie spied Moxie sniffing an object where the armoire had been and slid off the chair. She quietly approached the cat and grabbed her, pinning her to the floor. Moxie squirmed out of her grasp and scampered away, but left behind the item.

Sophie picked it up. "Daddy, look what I found. Can I keep it?"

With the sofa in the desired location, Jan held out her hand to the child. "Sophie, sweetie, can I have it, please?"

"I...I had to get off the chair." She gave the envelope to Jan while looking at Hatch and biting her bottom lip.

"Okay, honey."

Jan turned over the envelope and inhaled sharply. "It's addressed to me. In Bryan's handwriting." Her hands shook and the room spun. Slumped onto the black sofa, she stared at the envelope.

"Do you want me to open it?" Hatch sat on the edge of the seat beside her.

"No. I have to."

Using her thumb, she tore open the envelope and

removed a single sheet of paper. The words seemed to merge. She blinked.

> *January, 11*
> *Dear Jan:*
> *When you read this I'll be miles away. I couldn't tell you face-to-face*
> *what I was planning. Please forgive me for being such a coward.*
> *It's got nothing to do with us—but I know it will affect you. Something*
> *happened at work and I have to leave town. I still love you but I can't get*
> *married at this time. Sell the rest of my things and don't let Mama bug you*
> *too much.*
> *Love, Bryan*
> *P.S. Please don't try to find me.*

The paper fluttered out of her hands and floated to the carpet.

Hatch retrieved it. "Do you mind if I read it?"

Shocked into silence, Jan shook her head.

After Hatch read it, he folded the letter and slipped it back into the envelope. "He orchestrated his disappearance."

Jan stared into the distance.

"Did he have to leave because of the money?" Hatch set the envelope on the sofa.

Shaking off the numbing fog holding her captive, she grabbed the envelope scrunched it, and threw it onto the carpet. "Reports at the time accused him of embezzling funds from the insurance company where he worked, but I don't believe he did." At another time, she'd tell Hatch about The Thugs at her house searching for a ledger. They certainly didn't mention anything about money.

Jan pointed to the wad of paper. "I wonder how it got under the armoire? Maybe Bryan placed it in front of something on one of the shelves and it fell off. Maybe—I don't know. I can't think straight."

Moxie raced into the room, followed by Sophie. The cat pounced on the paper ball and tried to pick it up in her paws. She moved it back and forth, back and forth, across the carpet.

"Moxie, you little troublemaker. Did you hide it under the armoire? She loves to jump onto the shelves and could have knocked it off." Jan rescued the envelope from Moxie.

"Mystery solved?"

"Probably. His letter confirms my suspicions. He planned his disappearance, but why couldn't he tell me in person?"

Still unsteady and light-headed, Jan sat again.

Sophie ignored the cat and stepped toward the sofa. "It's okay, Jan." She patted Jan's knee. "My daddy's here. He helps people."

Jan smiled at Sophie and kissed her forehead.

"Thanks, sweetie. I know your daddy wants to help."

"This business with the letter has sort of put a damper on things. Sophie and I don't have to stay."

"Nonsense. I want you to stay. I'm fine. Who's ready for lunch?" Jan headed to the kitchen and glanced out the doors to the patio. The bowl of salad almost slipped from her fingers. She could be wrong about Bryan. Maybe The Thugs thought he left the money with her and she buried it under the tree.

CHAPTER 32

The lasagna had been a success. *Thank you, Delaney.* Jan carried the dishes to the kitchen, and Hatch cleared the other items from the table.

"I'll load the dishwasher later." Jan squatted to be at Sophie's eye level. "Your daddy says you like to paint. I have a surprise for you. Let's go upstairs."

The child looked to Hatch for confirmation, then took Jan's hand as they climbed the stairs.

When Jan showed Sophie the array of acrylic paints she'd prepared, her eyes widened and she said, "Ooh, are they all for me?"

"Yes, sweetie. Let me put this old T-shirt over your clothes."

Jan chose acrylics because oils would be too messy and watercolors not dramatic enough. She found five old eight-by-ten canvases and set her tabletop easel on a sturdy TV tray.

"I'm ready." Sophie selected a brush and swirled blobs of paint on the palette together, creating a variety of colors. Her fascination with the process almost superseded her joy at spreading paint on the canvas. Several canvases later Sophie had used up most of the paint.

"I think that's all for today. Maybe you can come back another time." Jan rescued the palette.

"Daddy, can I?"

"We'll see."

"Anyone for ice cream?" Jan placed the brushes in a tub of   soapy   water.

"Me, me." Sophie jumped up and down.

"Wash hands first. Hatch, will you help her?"

"Come here, honey." He picked her up and held her over the sink.

When most traces of paint had disappeared, Jan removed Sophie's T-shirt and everyone scampered down the stairs. She scooped ice cream into waffle cones and then dipped them in the chocolate sauce. Three satisfied customers sat around the kitchen table. Sophie couldn't quite finish hers which she handed to Hatch. Squealing with delight, she took off after Moxie again.

"Poor Moxie hasn't had this much exercise in years." Jan grinned.

"Sophie, be careful with the cat."

"They'll be fine. Moxie can always hide under the bed when she's had enough."

Hatch cleared his throat. "What's the verdict on Sophie's painting?"

Placing the container of chocolate sauce in the refrigerator gave Jan time to compose her thoughts. "Remember, I'm not an expert on child development and their artistic capabilities, but I'll give you my impressions. First, Sophie loves to paint and has a good sense of color. True, she used unconventional colors for objects, but she chose a different color for various items. She identified what she painted, and the objects look realistic. The figures even have five fingers on their hands."

"Yeah. She often draws people and animals."

"My best advice would be to surround her with different media and let her experiment to her heart's content. Oh, and never make her paint or color in the lines."

"That's one negative thing I remember from my early school days. I couldn't stay in the lines to save my life, so consequently never learned to appreciate or enjoy art." He shuddered. "I don't want Sophie to suffer from those restrictions. Thanks for taking the time to do this."

"It's been my pleasure."

They were quiet for a moment, then Hatch stood. "I don't hear Sophie."

He hurried into the living room and stopped. Index finger to his lips, he motioned Jan to join him. She peeked around him into the room. Sophie slept on the new sofa, with a throw rug she'd taken from the chair covering her little body, and a gray cat curled at her feet.

"Would you like a mug of coffee? Sorry, I don't have the ingredients for a London Fog." Jan whispered.

Hatch followed her back to the kitchen. "Not to worry. Coffee's fine."

Jan made two mugs of coffee and set them on the table. The nutty aroma replaced the faint leftover whiffs of the cheesy lasagna. She sipped her drink while Hatch stirred cream into his.

"I noticed a thin scar on your neck."

Jan touched the area. "Yeah, the cut healed quickly and it doesn't bother me."

"I have a question and I hope I don't make another faux pas. I noticed you always sit straight, no slouching, and I think even if you'd used those plastic discs, you couldn't have moved the armoire by yourself. Am I right?"

Very observant, Mr. Hatcher. There was no reason to keep her medical history from him. She set down her mug and clasped her hands in her lap. Although the surgeries happened a long time ago, discussing them still had the power to reduce her to a scared little girl, often teased by classmates, and always trying to catch up on missed school work.

"As a young toddler, I was diagnosed with severe scoliosis. I had a *C* curve in the thoracic region. My spine needed to be straightened so my lungs, chest cavity, and spine could develop properly. I had my first surgery at age five." She continued to explain the reason for the many surgeries she had and the limitations they necessitated. No contact sports. No rough and tumble play. "At age twelve, I had spinal fusion surgery to keep my spine straight. The vertebrae were fused by using bone taken from my hip. I won't bore you with a long explanation, but basically, the bones are welded together and have no flexibility."

"And the rods?"

"They're still in my back. The surgeon decided to leave them in situ. They don't hurt. My only limitation is I can't bend at the waist or twist my torso. Nor can I lift or move heavy objects"

He stared at her for a couple of seconds. "That's a lot of trauma for someone so young to endure."

"Yep." Suddenly, a wave of childhood memories overwhelmed her, thrusting her recent dream to the forefront of her mind. She frowned and bit her bottom lip.

"Hey, what's the matter? Have I inadvertently stuck my foot in again?"

She shook her head. "No, just resurrecting my past."

He reached across the table and took her hand. She recalled when they first met and the warmth of his hand had surprised her. She raised her gaze to his and for a moment forgot that he had frequently suggested counseling and she'd rebuffed his offers, maybe even rudely at times. But now she wanted his guidance and attention.

"Tell me."

Jan described her disastrous first year of school. "A group of four girls teased me every chance they got." She blinked, determined not to shed any tears. "They made up a song that I'd forgotten until it featured in a recent dream."

"What was the song? Get it all out." His voice held notes of tender sincerity.

She closed her eyes and whispered the words.

> *"Here comes Janyth, here comes Janyth.*
> *She has a crooked back and an ugly smile.*
> *We always catch her when we chase her*
> *Because she can't run a mile, she can't run a mile."*

The next thing she knew, Hatch stood over her and wrapped his arms around her. "That must have been devastating. I can't imagine how you survived." He scooted a chair closer and sat beside her.

"My middle sister was in second grade. I hadn't told anyone about the girls, but one day toward the end of the year, Delaney's class and my class were on the playground at the same time. She heard the song and saw the group chasing me." Jan smiled. "She waylaid them, and I don't know what she said, but she waved her arms about, pointed at them, and stuck her hands on her hips as a final gesture. They never bothered me again. To this day she won't divulge what she said."

"I'm glad she had your back, um, protected you."

"Me too." Jan frowned. After the incident, Delaney showed more concern and maybe realized life as spoiled little Jan wasn't all cake and cookies. "She might have threatened the group with our older sister, Teagan, who was in eighth grade and had a well-earned reputation as the best athlete in middle school."

"Why do you think you dreamt about the incident?"

Jan pursed her lips. Why? Aha. "I recently chatted with Bryan's mother. Out of left field, she mentioned Bryan didn't believe I had scoliosis. I doubt Bryan said that, but I guess it stuck in my subconscious."

"I'm sure reliving that time in your life has been painful, but cathartic, too. Right?"

Jan nodded. "Yeah." Relief covered her in a comfortable gossamer mantle. She folded her arms on the table and rested her head on them. Her tears had dried up and the gash in her heart began to mend. The song no longer had the power to cripple her spirit. Then she giggled and raised her head. "Oh, my goodness. The ugly smile line. I'd lost several front teeth, upper and lower. My new incisors were crooked and I had a difficult time pronouncing words."

"You have a beautiful smile, now."

"Thanks to the orthodontist." Jan straightened and giggled again.

"What now?"

"A while ago you noticed the little scar on my neck. Well, it's minuscule compared to those on my back. Since I'm in a confessing mode, I'll expound. You can imagine how they influenced what I wore as a teenager. I hated wearing a bathing suit. I avoided sundresses. My low self-confidence was shattered when my peers teased me." She shrugged. "As a young adult, I'd overcome the embarrassment, but some men I dated were repulsed by the scars. My social life suffered so I focused on my painting." Up until now, Jan had stared at the cabinets. She turned to Hatch. "Whew. That was a loaded speech."

He held her hand and seemed to be processing her words. "I'm honored that you shared those intimate details with me. I can't imagine what you experienced. All I can say is, you've triumphed over your past." Running a finger across the little scar on her neck, he swallowed hard. "I admire you so much."

A faint voice from the den interrupted their conversation.

"Daddy, Daddy, where are you?"

Hatch planted a kiss on the top of Jan's head and hurried to the den. He picked up Sophie who wrapped her legs around his torso and arms around his neck.

Jan placed her hands over her heart. Sophie must feel so safe cradled in her daddy's strong arms.

"I think it's time for us to go."

"No, Daddy. My paintings."

"Let's collect them." Jan headed to the stairs. "Hatch, you must save them. When she's famous one day you can say you have her very first masterpieces."

"They will be displayed very proudly." He followed and Jan handed him one of the canvases.

"Why do you have so much paint?" Sophie surveyed the studio from her high perch in Hatch's arms.

"That's what I do, sweetie. I paint pictures for people

and they pay me."

"And remember, honey, I told you she paints pictures for children's books. She painted the pictures of *Mr. Caterpillar*."

Sophie stared wide-eyed at Jan. "Show me. Paint Mr. Caterpeeper for me."

"I can't do that." For Hatch's benefit, she added, "*Mr. Caterpillar* is a copyrighted figure. But I can do this." She turned and opened a huge full-length cabinet with narrow shelves. "I can show you these."

Pulling out several sheets from protective layers, Jan spread them on the counter and removed the coverings. "These are the original paintings for one of the books."

Sophie and Hatch peered at them.

"It *is* Mr. Caterpeeper." Sophie pointed and grinned.

"These are magnificent."

When Jan carefully returned the originals to the cabinet, Hatch set Sophie down and told her to get her coat in the den. Jan and Hatch carried Sophie's canvases downstairs.

"I still don't think she believes I painted the pictures she sees in her book." Jan rested two canvases against the wall beside Sophie's other pictures.

"It's probably a little too abstract for her. After all, to her books magically appear in the library or bookstore." He helped Sophie button her coat and then put on his jacket. "When will the book about the ferret be published?"

"Flossie? February, 15. I'll give Sophie a signed copy."

Holding one of her paintings, Sophie skipped to the front door. "Come on, Daddy."

Hatch arched an eyebrow. "Her birthday's in March."

"Good timing. Thanks for helping today. For the furniture and for listening. You are a good therapist, Mr.

Hatcher."

"I appreciate your trust in me. You are a strong woman."

Jan waited until Hatch had secured Sophie and her canvases in the Jeep then she closed the door and walked to the kitchen. She meant what she said. Hatch had helped her expel the childhood tormentors from her soul and had given her the courage to tell him how the scars affected her younger years.

Whistling random notes, she rinsed dishes and loaded the dishwasher. Her heart felt lighter and her world looked brighter. Hatch was right. Talking about her issues had helped immensely.

She'd enjoyed the interesting day and wouldn't mind a repeat even if Hatch's conversation and actions exhibited no hint of romance.

CHAPTER 33

During the ride home, Sophie indulged in her latest interest—identifying logos she recognized. "I see McDonald's. And there's H. E. B. That's a big grocery store, isn't it, Daddy?"

"Yes, honey."

"Why doesn't it have a real name? Why is it only letters?"

"I don't know but I will find out. What else can you see?" The daycare teacher recommended the activity to encourage kids to read.

"Um, there's Home Depooooo." She exaggerated the last syllable and then chuckled. "That's a funny word. It should be de-pot."

"It is unusual." Was it too early to tell her about silent letters? He stopped at a red light and adjusted the rearview mirror to see her. She was growing up so quickly.

Suddenly, she squealed. "Daddy, there's the man. He's scaring me."

"What man?"

"The man with no hair. He scratched on my window."

The light turned green and Hatch drove a few feet before her words registered. "Where is he?"

"In that car." She pounded on the window. "The black one next to us."

There were no vehicles ahead of him. He checked the side mirrors. A dark sedan hung back a few yards. It might be similar to the one at the park when the bald guy threatened Jan. He slowed. The car turned right at the next intersection. Hatch stopped, did a U-turn, and followed it. No dark sedan in sight. He drove around the block, up one street then down another, but he never saw the vehicle again.

Arriving home frustrated and angry, he parked in the garage and was about to slam his door, when he took a breath. He couldn't allow his anger to spill over onto Sophie. He took her out of her car seat. "Are you all right, honey?"

She nodded but frowned. "I told you I saw a man that night."

"Yes, Sophie, and remember we have a security system so no one can get in through your bedroom window. Okay?"

"Okay."

He helped her carry her canvases inside and then hung up their jackets. "Let's put this beautiful picture in your room."

"Yes, Daddy, but this one's for *your* room."

Hatch took the canvas Sophie handed him and beamed. A purple tree, blue sun, and stick figures of him holding her hand.

"Thank you. I'll look at it every night before I go to sleep and think of you. I'll find a place for the other pictures downstairs." He found the perfect spot for two canvases in the kitchen, and the last one he'd hang in the living room. In the meantime, he placed it on the coffee table. Since they'd had a substantial lunch, he took a container of soup from the freezer and set it in the sink.

Sophie pulled her box of colors and coloring book from her toy basket and sat at the kitchen table. A fat blue crayon in her little hand, she colored across the sky of an animal picnic scene. "Daddy, I like to paint. Can I have paints like Jan let me use? Maybe for my birthday?"

"That's a good idea. Next time we go shopping, we'll look at paints."

While she remained occupied, he phoned Jan. The bald man had a connection to her. When she answered, he told her what Sophie had seen.

"That's terrible. I imagine she was scared. Do you think it was the man from the park?"

"I didn't see him but the car sure was similar."

She hesitated. "Do you have some time? I have a lot to tell you about bald men."

"Go ahead." He was not prepared for what she shared. Two bald men named Harold and Tom wanted information about Bryan. They'd threatened her, harassed her. Even tied her up and searched her home. And may have dug up a tree in her backyard. "No wonder you looked like you had cinder blocks on your shoulders, weighing you down. Dear Jan, you told the authorities, right?"

"Yes. My eldest sister is a police officer, and the sergeant I've been communicating with is a friend of hers."

"And?"

"These men are evasive. They don't leave fingerprints. I don't know their last names. Sergeant Voss has no leads, and since my home invasion event, I haven't heard from Harold or Tom."

Hatch opened the back door to let in cool air to calm his ire. "The bald man in the car might not be either Harold or Tom, but what if they followed us to intimidate me? Maybe thinking I could persuade you to give them what they want."

"I'll pass this information on to Voss. Did you manage to get the license plate number?"

"No, sorry."

"In case the man was either Harold or Tom, don't take any chances."

"I reassured Sophie today that no one could enter her bedroom window. I will set the alarm even when we're home during the day."

"How about daycare? Who's authorized to pick up Sophie?"

"Only Margaret and me. They have a strict protocol in place. I think she's safe there."

"Good."

"I suppose there's nothing else I can do."

"I'm not letting them interfere in my life."

"Good advice." He closed the door and sat at the table with Sophie. "I enjoyed our day with you. So did Sophie."

"I did, too. Goodnight."

There might not be anything Hatch could do, but his PI friend might have some ideas. He called Garrett and left a message.

Later that evening, when Sophie selected a bedtime story for Hatch to read, she chose the *Mr. Caterpillar* book. But instead of listening to the familiar words, Sophie concentrated on the pictures. She even prevented Hatch from turning the pages a time or two.

"Look, Daddy. That's Jan's painting."

A caterpillar dressed in a carpenter's apron holding various tools in his numerous hands constructing a multi-storied house. After Hatch completed the story— as much as Sophie would let him—she closed the book and cuddled next to him.

A small sigh escaped. "I like Jan. And I like painting."

Hatch cradled her for a while then kissed the top of her head. "I like Jan too." Tomorrow after church, he'd ask Jan's advice about purchasing items for artist Sophie. She might agree to accompany them on their shopping expedition.

After listening to Sophie's prayers and tucking her in, Hatch retreated to his office. He settled at his desk, worked for several hours, and then accessed his schedule on the computer. Valentine's Day was around the corner. He tapped his pen on the desk in sync with his accelerated heartbeat. He'd arrange a romantic outing for Jan. Which meant, he'd need a babysitter. Call Margaret. Nope. Hmm. He'd ask someone else. At church tomorrow.

Seated in his comfortable recliner, Hatch sipped his London Fog and turned on the TV. He couldn't find anything decent to watch and was about to turn it off when the doorbell rang. And rang. He hurried to open the door before Sophie awoke.

Margaret stood on the porch. "Can I come in?"

"Of course." He followed her to the living room and muted the TV.

"I came by earlier this afternoon but you weren't here."

She appeared calm and in control so Hatch sat and answered immediately. "Sophie and I had lunch with Jan."

"Where?"

"At her home."

Margaret stepped to the window. "I should have known." She glanced at the coffee table where Hatch had placed Sophie's painting. "What's this? Did Sophie paint it at that woman's house?"

Warning bells sounded in his head and he stood. "Margaret, come sit down, please." He gestured toward an armchair. "Yes, Jan provided several canvases and a palette of paint. Sophie had a blast."

"Does Jan think she can weasel her way close to you by doing fun activities with your daughter?" Margaret sat on the edge of the seat. "What about all the fun things I planned for her over the years? Don't they count?"

The conversation and Margaret's demeanor quickly took a downward turn. Since this was the first time he'd spoken with her after declaring he only loved her as a sister, he marshaled all his counselor jargon and expertise and moved another armchair closer to her. "I can see you're upset, Maggie. You know I appreciate all you've done for us." He paused, eyes on her facial expression. "I take full responsibility for not recognizing that you wanted more from me than friendship. I didn't see what was right before my eyes. I am so sorry if I misled you in any way."

Margaret lowered her head and clasped her hands.

Hatch waited for her to respond, and when she didn't, he continued. "I apologize for taking our friendship for granted by asking you to take care of Sophie so often. She loves you."

"But that's not enough." She raised her head and stared at him, her blue eyes brimming with tears and her face flushed.

"I can't give you what you want, dear Maggie.

Please accept my sincerest apology."

A long minute crawled by during which her breathing returned to normal. She rose and pulled her car keys from her jacket pocket.

Hatch stood, too.

"I still don't understand how you failed to read the signs. Day after day, month after month." She walked toward the front door and turned. "You should close your practice, Hatch. Go find a job you're more qualified for."

With that jab, she opened the door and slammed it behind her.

His mouth gaped and his hands curled into fists. For a split second, her statement irked him, but then reality took over and he relaxed. His off-the-cuff idea of returning to cattle ranching might not be far-fetched. Margaret seemed to agree with him.

Hatch locked the door and set the alarm.

CHAPTER 34

Winter vacated South Texas for a couple of days. When Jan left the church building after the service, she didn't need to wear her coat. She carried it over her arm and clutched her Bible in her hand. Since Hatch had participated in the forum of speakers for the service, she had not spoken to him yet and scanned the crowd for his dark hair and navy sweater.

Small, warm fingers grasped her free hand and Jan glanced down at Sophie's cute face staring up at her.

"Hi, Jan, Paint Lady."

"Paint Lady. Is that all you can say about me?"

Jan ached to pick her up but couldn't because of the coat and Bible in her arms. She squatted down by the child instead.

"You do have lots of paint."

"You're right, sweetie. Did Daddy hang up your pictures?"

Nodding, she turned when someone called her name. "Bye, Paint Lady." Braids bobbing, she skipped away.

As Jan stood, she bumped into a woman standing behind her, knocking her arm. The woman lost her grip on her Bible and it fell to the ground.

"I'm so sorry. Let me help you." Jan picked up the Bible and a few of the loose papers scattered about.

"That's okay. No harm done."

At the sound of Margaret's voice, Jan grabbed the last page, placed the papers inside the Bible, and handed it to her. "Sorry again, Margaret."

"Thank you."

To search the group for Hatch, Jan took a step sideways. Crunch. Another piece of paper. She picked it up. "Wait Margaret, here's—"

But Margaret had disappeared into the crowd.

Shrugging, Jan glanced at the paper. Writing covered the parchment. The same set of words repeated over and over. Some printed; some in cursive; some in fancy calligraphy. Large, small. Her hand shook and the paper fluttered as she read: *Margaret Hatcher; Maggie Hatcher; Mrs. Hatcher; Mrs. KC. Hatcher.*

She recognized the doodling of a woman in love, a woman dreaming of or planning a wedding. Hadn't she done the same thing with a boy's name in high school? But she couldn't remember doing it with Bryan Buchanan's name. Grimacing, she took a deep breath and shoved the paper into her pants pocket.

Retrieving her phone from her purse, she texted Delaney.

Please call. Please.

She stared at the phone and almost dropped it when Hatch touched her arm. Pivoting, she glared at him.

"Want to join us for lunch? Sophie wants spaghetti."

"Ooh, my favorite." Margaret came up to Hatch carrying Sophie. "Can I join you?"

Irrational thoughts seized control of Jan's mind. She couldn't endure an hour with Hatch and Margaret together. "I can't. Thanks anyway. I'm waiting for my sister to text me." Before he could respond, she fled to her car. Too late, she remembered she still had the piece of paper and turned, but Margaret and Hatch were out of sight.

Delaney didn't call. Jan assumed she might still be at her church service. *Another meal alone.* Jan stopped at a restaurant far away from Deer Park.

Eating food she didn't remember ordering, she analyzed her emotional reaction to finding that crucial piece of paper. Betrayal ate at her soul. But upon further scrutiny, she couldn't blame anyone but herself. Hatch had not led her on. He was happy to see her, had invited her to supper, and accepted her invitation for lunch the previous day. When she explained her medical issues, he didn't shy away. Had she read too much into it all?

But then the ogre in the room reared its head. Jan recalled Hatch's exact answer to her question about Margaret. *She is just a friend. I am not interested in her romantically.*

Jan leaned back and sipped her iced tea. Two possibilities. Hatch lied, or Margaret lived in a fantasy world. Either way, she couldn't maintain a relationship with Hatch based only on friendship. Too much to comprehend at one time gave her indigestion. She pushed her plate away and paid the bill.

Moxie welcomed her home. "I can always count on you, girl." She flopped onto her new sofa and picked up the cat.

Hatch deserved a spot right next to Bryan.

In her past.

CHAPTER 35

The next day, Jan made a copy of Bryan's letter and took it to Marybeth. She hesitated before inviting Jan in. Once in the living room, Jan explained how she'd found the letter and gave the copy to Marybeth.

The woman sank onto the sofa and read the words. "How can I know you didn't write this?" She waved the paper about.

"Don't you recognize his handwriting?"

Marybeth nodded and clutched the letter to her chest. Tears pooled in her eyes. "Why didn't he write to me?" Sobbing, she bent her legs and curled up in a fetal position.

The last time Jan had tried to offer sympathy, she'd been chased out of the house, but she knelt beside Marybeth anyway. "I'm so sorry." No negative reaction from the woman. "He will contact us one day, I'm sure." Still no response. "Can I get you a cup of coffee?" Marybeth always had a pot made.

"Yes, please."

Jan straightened and headed to the kitchen. The

house was reasonably tidy, and even the sink was empty. She poured a mug of coffee and took it to Marybeth.

She lowered her legs and took the mug. "Thanks. I'm okay now. You don't have to stay any longer."

"Call if you need anything." Jan hurried home and left a message for Voss. He probably wouldn't ask for a copy of Bryan's letter, but she wanted him to know about it.

On the way to the gallery, Voss returned her call. "At least your belief is confirmed. He did plan his disappearance. However, he doesn't admit to leaving anything with you. Even if you shared the letter with Harold and Tom, it wouldn't help in locating the items. Have you heard from them recently?"

"No. It's a relief to be free of them. Thanks for calling, sergeant." Jan parked outside the gallery and entered Pat's office.

"Hey, *mija*. How's the portrait coming?"

"I might finish it today. Tomorrow at the latest."

"Good. I have another artist who wants to rent the studio next week."

"I'll be out of the way by Wednesday." Jan passed many of her displayed paintings as she headed toward the back of the gallery. The studio had several windows and a skylight which provided a perfect indoor environment for an artist. She slipped on her smock, prepared her pallet, and sat on the stool.

She was in the perfect location doing a job she

loved, yet, her shoulders sagged and a heavy lump sat on her heart. Bryan left because of a work-related problem but never contacted her or his mother. Hatch had acted as if he was interested in her, yet Margaret was always in the background. Would Jan ever be able to hold onto a man?

What about Richard? She studied his portrait. He was a fun guy, and she enjoyed his company. But she couldn't quite pinpoint why he wasn't Mr. Right. In an attempt to shrug off the disillusionment, Jan picked up a brush. She added more shadows to Richard's face, produced the precise color for his eyes, and did justice to his magnificent smile. Before she painted his glasses, she stepped back to evaluate her work. A good balance of colors in the background which complimented his suit. His facial features were perfect. And they reminded her of someone.

A slow, menacing force nibbled at the nape of her neck. She shook her head and stood on unsteady legs. No, it couldn't be. Her imagination must be on steroids. She blinked and studied his face again. Without his hair painted yet, he could be bald. He could be—

Jan's blood ran cold and she shivered. With a few adjustments, the portrait could be of Harold or Tom. Was Richard another brother? She rubbed her temples. Every time she'd seen the two men there had never been a third male with them. Were her eyes deceiving her? No. The resemblance was too profound.

Pacing in the small studio, Jan let her thoughts run

rampant. The only time she'd seen all three men together was the day The Thugs invaded her house. They'd gained access when Richard was leaving. Had that been prearranged? The event was etched into her memory. Richard came inside because he had a coughing fit. Legit or contrived? He'd received and responded to a text before he headed to the front door. Had he been communicating with Harold or Tom? The only way they could enter her home without setting off the alarm was when Richard opened the door. Another incident came to mind—the chance meeting the day he jogged past her house. She'd been so wrapped up in his desire to have his portrait painted that she hadn't noticed he wasn't sweating. And Richard paid with cash. He left no credit card number to trace.

Seated again, Jan reviewed her options. Continue with the portrait and chalk up the resemblance to chance. Or, contact Sergeant Voss and explain her suspicions.

One last study of the portrait and Jan made up her mind. She scrambled for her phone in her purse, noted several missed calls from Hatch, and dialed Voss's number. She left a message, and while waiting for his call, wrapped up her palette and tidied the studio.

Voss called thirty minutes later and Jan explained her conviction.

"You've been face-to-face with all three men, and if you think Richard is part of the family, then I believe you. What's his last name?"

Jan had to think back to their first meeting. "Um, starts with a *C*. Car…Carson."

"And is there anything at your house that might have his fingerprints on it?"

"Let me think." He'd last been in her home almost two weeks ago. She'd washed the glass he drank from, and wiped the table, but… "Yes. I kept the envelope that contained his cash down payment."

"I'll come by today to get it. Do you have his phone number? Can you invite him to your house and I'll arrange for—"

"I have a better idea. I told him he'd have to come to the studio when I concentrated on his face. He's expecting that call."

"Good. Set up the meeting for tomorrow. Give me the address of the studio."

Jan provided the details. "What time should I have him come?"

"When does the gallery open?"

"Ten o'clock."

"Ask him to come at ten-thirty. I'll have a couple of plain-clothed officers in the gallery."

"Okay." Jan blew out a breath.

"Are you all right?"

"No, but I will be when Richard is arrested and you question him about Harold and Tom."

She drove home, avoiding the highway and the traffic which she knew would only add to her frustration.

Safe in her house, she dumped her purse on the kitchen counter and plodded into the den. Seated on her new sofa, she crossed her arms. Then she jumped up. The sofa reminded her of Hatch. Hatch who'd called her many times and left messages she'd ignore. Hatch who'd betrayed her.

Jan picked up Moxie who snuggled against her and settled at the kitchen table. No Hatch and no Richard. She glanced out the window. Her love life was as bleak as the gray sky.

~*~*~

Richard agreed to visit the studio at ten-thirty. Voss had introduced the two officers who'd act as customers and reminded Jan he'd be stationed at the rear of the building.

With the portrait in the middle of the small studio, Jan placed a chair close by and unwrapped her pallet, all to convince Richard the sitting was genuine. She checked her watch a dozen times and attempted a welcoming smile when he finally arrived. "Hey, Richard. I'm glad you could make it. I missed you at church."

"Sorry. My trip out of town lasted longer than I'd planned." He stood in front of the portrait. "Wow. This is fantastic. My folks will love it."

"Good. Have a seat and I'll get my pallet ready." As she turned to the counter, the door opened, and one of the plain-clothed officers entered. Jan said, "Hi, Sandra. I have your picture ready."

Sandra played along. "Thanks so much for bringing it. Who's this handsome guy?"

The target beamed and held out his hand. "I'm Richard Carson. Did Jan paint your portrait, too?"

"No." She held open her jacket and exposed her police badge. "I'm Sergeant Diaz with the San Antonio Police Department and I have some questions for you, Mr. Carson."

"Questions? What's going on, Jan?"

Voss joined them in the studio, closed the door, and stood feet apart, looking every bit in charge.

"Mr. Carson, do you have any identification on you?" Sandra asked.

"No."

"Not even a driver's license?"

"Uh, no."

Jan toyed with the plastic wrap from her pallet. "How did you get here? Where's your truck?"

"My pickup's in the shop. I took a taxi."

"Wrong," Voss said. "I saw you arrive in a black Ford pickup. I checked the plate number and it's not registered to Richard Carson."

Richard's confident posture deflated and he cocked his head. "Okay, so you got me."

"Please stand and put your hands behind your back." Sandra had her cuffs ready. "Richard *Jennings,* I'm arresting you for providing false information to the police." She secured the cuffs around his wrists.

He looked at Jan and clicked his tongue. "Jan, how

could you?"

"Richard, how could *you*? You're a liar and a…a…" She turned her back on him and folded her arms.

"What will you do with my portrait?"

"I'll show you." She grabbed a utility knife and slashed across the canvas, cutting his face in two. Heart heavy with disappointment, she ran from the studio.

CHAPTER 36

Another call went to Jan's voicemail. Why hadn't she contacted him? Hatch parked beside a Ford Escape, dark blue with white rims which briefly took his mind off Jan. The tenants of the small office complex had problems with people from the nearby apartments using their private parking lot. He knew what vehicles were usually there, and the old Ford was not one of them. He took down the license plate number in case he needed it.

Climbing the flight of stairs, Hatch shook his head. Strange car forgotten, he thought about the last time he saw Jan. After church. He invited her to lunch, and Margaret walked up behind him. But she'd seemed distracted even before Maggie arrived.

He unlocked his office door and suddenly two men shoved him inside and closed the door. "What the—?"

An arm encircled his neck and a hand covered his mouth. "Don't struggle and don't call out."

The other man stood in front of him. A bald man Hatch recognized from the park. "By now you probably know we've been paying a lot of attention to your girlfriend, Jan."

Hatch pulled the hand away from his mouth. "You must be Harold and Tom."

"I'm Harold, Mr. Hatcher. Tom will choke the life out of you if you struggle. Your girl is becoming a big problem. Do you know she's responsible for the arrest of our cousin?"

"Your cousin?"

"Ahh, so she hasn't told you."

If only she had communicated with him.

The arm around his neck tightened and Tom said, "We want you to pass on a message to her."

"Yeah. Tell her we know Bryan is back in San Antonio, and if he contacts her, she must let us know. We'll tell her how to contact us."

"Wait, he's back? How do you know?" Is that why Jan hadn't returned his calls?

Harold raised an eyebrow. "We have our sources."

"What if I refuse?" Hatch had to wheedle a bit more information from them.

Tom removed his arm, swung Hatch around, and punched him in the solar plexus.

Hatch doubled over.

"We know where you live. We know where your cute little girl goes to daycare. By the way, I love the pretty lilac curtains in her bedroom." Harold chuckled, a dry humorless sound.

Gulping in air, Hatch straightened. Fury fueled his

muscles and he ran full-tilt at Tom, but he stepped out of the way, and Hatch hit an armchair.

"We'll leave you now. If you know what's good for you and Jan, you'll pass on our message." Tom opened the door and both men left the office.

Still struggling to breathe, Hatch hurried after them but they'd disappeared. He ran to a window at the end of the hall, and sure enough, they were backing out of the parking area in the blue Ford. He returned to his office and slumped into his desk chair. Who was the cop Jan had been reporting to? She'd mentioned him briefly. Voss, yes.

Hatch knew which substation served their area of San Antonio and located their number. He was fortunate Sergeant Voss was available. After explaining what had happened and repeating the message they wanted to pass on to Jan, he added the vehicle details.

"That's helpful. I'll issue a BOLO on the car."

"They mentioned Jan was responsible for the arrest of their cousin."

"Correct. I believe you met Richard."

"Yes, at our church." The scoundrel. "Jan is not answering my calls. Could you pass on the message, please?"

"Definitely. Thank you for the information, but let us handle this, Mr. Hatcher. You stay out of it."

CHAPTER 37

The morning began with a phone call from Sergeant Voss. Jan sat at the kitchen table, coffee momentarily forgotten, anticipating good news.

"Jan, I have two things to tell you. First, Bryan might be back in San Antonio."

"What? How do you know?"

"I can't reveal the details. Second, Harold and Tom accosted Mr. Hatcher in his office yesterday."

Jan drew in a shuddering breath. "Is he all right?"

"Yes. They threatened him and gave him a message for you. If Bryan makes contact, you must notify one of them."

"I…I don't know what to say." She wanted to call Hatch. She wanted to see him.

"There's more. Richard requested an attorney right away. He's given us nothing. We've done a background check using his real name. He lives in Houston and works for Woodward Insurance."

And I fell for his act. "Of course he does. Wow. Bryan's information must be detrimental to the company for three men to be after it."

"The evidence we have supports that supposition. Remember, Harold or Tom will contact you. You need to remain vigilant."

"I will." Voss ended the call and Jan poured out her cold coffee. Bryan back in San Antonio? Would he contact her? She stared at her phone. The Thugs threatened Hatch. Voss reported he was okay. Jan shoved her phone into her pocket. She didn't want to speak to Hatch, yet. She needed more time for her emotions to adapt to the new reality. If she spoke to him, she might lose control and say something she'd later regret.

Jan had no desire to work in her studio. Instead, she visited Delaney who had a new pet-sitting gig in a nearby neighborhood. The ranch-style house sat on a corner lot with massive oak trees shading the front yard. When Jan rang the doorbell, deep-throated woofs responded from inside.

The door opened a smidge. "Let me leash the dogs, then you can come in. Otherwise, they will lick you to death."

Woofs and whines continued, and then Delaney opened the door. She held the leashes for three huge dogs, all sitting at her feet. "They are well trained, but the doorbell sends them into a frenzy."

Jan held out her hand to each dog and patted their heads. "Are they bloodhounds?"

"Yeah. Droopy jowls, sad eyes, and long ears.

Come to the kitchen. I'm in the middle of preparing their special food." The dogs followed her and she ushered them outside.

Delaney seemed to be enjoying her new job, and Jan didn't want to spoil her mood by sharing anything that happened during the past couple of days. Later, Delaney made paninis and served them with a rich coleslaw. Trust her to have the ingredients on hand.

After lunch, Jan traveled to Boerne to apply the sealant to the two canvases she repaired. Mounted to take full advantage of the high ceiling, the large landscapes were perfect for the bank's entryway. Not even another artist would be able to locate the repairs Jan had made. Nathan held the ladder while she covered each patched area with sealant. "All done and ready for the grand opening on Friday."

Nathan waited for Jan to descend the ladder and then shook her hand. "Thank you again."

Beaming, she placed the supplies in her case. "I'm looking forward to Friday's event. See you then."

She spent the rest of the afternoon gathering materials and updating information for her accountant to prepare her Income Tax return.

~*~*~

The next morning, Jan dressed in her new bronze sweater and calf-length silk skirt with gold and bronze cascading swirls. The bank opening was scheduled for ten o'clock, and the parking area was almost full when she arrived. She hurried inside and stood with the throng of people gathered in the foyer.

Nathan Yeats stepped behind a small podium, tapped the microphone, and welcomed everyone. He introduced the staff, and to Jan's embarrassment, complimented her landscapes and beckoned her to the podium. Amid the applause, she surveyed the audience. She did a double-take. The man at the back looked like…Hatch. Jan swallowed and lowered her head.

A few minutes later, the photographer took several shots of her standing beneath her paintings. When the young woman moved to another subject, Jan searched for Nathan to say goodbye, but he was at the refreshment table, supervising the servers. She was going to leave anyway until Hatch approached her.

"You're a hard person to reach by phone."

"I've been busy. How did you know about the event?"

"I use a branch of this bank in San Antonio and they promoted the opening in their newsletter. When the article mentioned original Sullivan landscapes, I knew it had to be you."

"Why did you come?"

He deposited his glass and plate on a side table, took her by the arm, and moved away from the crowd.

"I need to talk to you. I think you've been avoiding me and I want to know why. You didn't return my calls. You ran away after church."

"I didn't run away. I've been…busy. I told you. These," Jan pointed to the paintings, "take time."

"I understand, but there's more to it. What have I done to incur your displeasure? There's something. I can sense it."

She leaned against a limestone column and stared at him. His eyes, accentuated by the blue shirt, were tender and concern etched lines on his brow.

Jan clasped her hands around her purse strap while a battalion of emotions fought for dominance in her heart. Disbelief, anxiety, hope, and anger. Anger won. She glared at him and grappled for control of her voice. "First of all Hatch, you must let me say what's on my mind. Please don't interrupt me." She sought his confirmation and continued after his nod. "Whenever we've been together you've left me with the impression that...that it was special, that I was someone you wanted to be with. I know you've been calling me recently and I've ignored your calls because I don't want to associate with people who lie to me."

"Whoa. I have many faults, but lying is not one of them."

"I'll contradict your statement. A few days ago we had a phone conversation. Your voice sounded sincere, but I couldn't interpret your body language." Would a face-to-face conversation have helped? Richard had done nothing but lie to her in person. "You said you weren't romantically interested in Margaret."

"That's the truth. She's a friend. No more." He hesitated.

Jan jumped into the gap. "Does she agree?"

"What do you mean? Has she said something to you?"

"She's dropped several hints. But last Sunday after church, I bumped into her and her Bible fell to the ground. I helped pick up the papers that had been inside." Jan reached into her purse and removed a crumpled sheet of paper. "I found this." She waved the page in front of Hatch.

He snatched it from her fingers.

An aura of calmness surrounded Jan and her anger gave way to sincere inquiry. "Hatch, this can only mean one thing. Margaret is either going to, or wants to, marry you. Which is it?"

Hatch's mouth fell open and he stared at the paper, then at Jan's face, and chuckled. "Jan, honey. This is not what you think."

Her anger returned and she folded her arms. "Really? I certainly don't think your duplicity is funny. Margaret's always in your company and has priority on your time."

"Jan, I have explained how Margaret helped me after Laura passed. We became close, and she misinterpreted that closeness. Last week, she admitted she's in love with me. I...I had no idea and apologized for giving her the impression her feelings were reciprocated."

Hatch's words hit Jan with the force of a two-by-four. She staggered backward, staring at him.

"As you can imagine, Margaret's angry with me. I

didn't tell her there's someone else I'm interested in. Very interested. She must have sensed my attraction to you." He held out a hand toward her.

Shaking her head, she ignored his gesture and turned away. She needed time. And space.

"Please, Jan, don't leave."

Something in his tone touched her heart and she looked at him.

"Jan, don't you know? I'm falling in love with you and these past several days have been complete agony."

Had she heard him correctly? She had to escape. Heading to the foyer, she glanced at a man and woman standing by the exit doors. She froze in place as she felt the blood drain from her face. The man looked like Bryan. A slimmer version with shoulder-length hair and a beard. He held her gaze. Yes. It was Bryan. Good thing Voss told her he might be in San Antonio, otherwise she would have fainted on the spot.

CHAPTER 38

Bryan cocked his head toward the doors and mouthed, "Meet us outside, please."

Jan nodded, waved to Nathan, and slipped out the doors. She had fantasized about this meeting for so long but now her many questions for Bryan tangled in her mind.

A large oak tree grew in a graveled area adjacent to the bank. The landscapers had placed two benches around a sunken garden of cacti. Bryan and the woman settled on the nearest bench, and Jan hurried to the other one before her wobbly knees gave out.

Her words organized themselves into coherent thoughts. "Why, Bryan, why did you leave? Why didn't you contact me?"

"I had my reasons, which I'll share with you later. First, I want to—"

"How did you know I'd be here today?" She remembered he liked to drag out a conversation and she needed quick answers.

"I've...we've been in town a week. This is

Amanda McKenzie, my girlfriend. She's here to support me. We followed you to Boerne and found out about the event."

Jan nodded to the redhead but addressed Bryan. "You've become good at subterfuge."

"I'm sorry Jan. I want to explain about the other thing."

"You mean the *disappearance* thing? Please go ahead. I've waited a long time to hear this story." She studied the man who'd made her life a misery. His face hadn't changed, maybe the hairline had receded some. The beard hid his weak chin but the long hair gave him a rakish air. As she stared at Bryan, this revised version of him became fuzzy as if in a mirage. He and Amanda floated off the bench.

Jan shook her head which didn't help. She was still reeling from Hatch's words. He loved her. And Bryan sat before her alive, and probably well. And he was about to answer the question that had been foremost in her mind for months. Her throat dried up. She swallowed despite the Saharan dune in her throat. "Hurry up, Bryan. Rain is in the forecast. Tell me why you left."

His account was nothing like Jan had imagined. The San Antonio branch of Woodward Insurance Company had been involved in shady business deals. He had tried to do the honorable thing by reporting the problems, but his actions were not appreciated. While searching for another job, his life had been threatened.

"When they said they'd come after you, too, Jan, I decided to leave town. I copied all the incrementing evidence onto a USB flash drive and hid it in the DVD storage binder I left at your house, in case someone from Woodward found me and searched me."

"Did you tell the police about the threat?"

"No. I didn't think they'd believe me because someone in my department manufactured evidence against me, as if I was involved in the fraud, and included an embezzlement charge. Naturally, I realize now I probably should have contacted the authorities."

"I'd heard about the embezzlement but knew you wouldn't have stolen anything. Why didn't you tell me? I didn't know, didn't have a clue."

"I couldn't tell you any more than I put in my letter. I thought you'd be safer if you didn't know any of the details, and if you didn't know my whereabouts. And I definitely couldn't tell Mama. She'd never have been able to keep it a secret."

"That's become quite a problem." Jan hugged herself to ward off the cold wind. Suddenly, Hatch appeared, placed his jacket around her shoulders, and sat beside her. "Thanks for the jacket. This is Bryan and his girlfriend." She'd forgotten her name but didn't care. "I only found your letter recently, but time and again, I tried to convince Marybeth you weren't dead. I told her about the items you came back for and the two occasions I received flowers. That was you, wasn't it?"

Bryan sighed. "Yes. I wanted you to know I still

thought of you."

"A card or letter included would have been nice."

"Sorry, again. I didn't think Mother would react that way." He hesitated. "I don't mean to hurt you—at least no more than I have already—but I... This is so hard. Even if I'd stayed I don't think..."

"I know. I don't think it would have worked out between us." She glanced at Hatch who smiled at her. She was grateful for his company and for not adding to the conversation.

"We can both move on. You know, leave the past behind us and forge ahead. That's something anyway."

They were silent for a moment.

"Move on, indeed." Erudite explanation from the usual reticent Bryan. He must have rehearsed that little description. At least, none of what he'd shared so far indicated Jan was to blame for his disappearance. It was comforting to have that confirmation. "Where have you been?"

"I drifted for a while, doing odd jobs. Then I moved to New York and met Amanda. I've been working for her father, sort of living under the radar." He slipped his arm around her shoulders. "Has anyone ever approached you or bothered you about my disappearance?"

Jan had to chuckle. "Yes. Two guys who call themselves Harold and Tom."

When Jan described the men, Bryan recognized them as employees and special friends of the insurance company's head of security.

"Did they hurt you?"

"No. They've harassed me, and even searched my house." Hatch drew her closer, and she whispered, "Thank you."

Bryan mumbled, "I'm so sorry. Did they want information about me?"

"Of course. They wanted to know where you were and what you might have given me before you left."

"How would they know I had any evidence?"

"While they were in my house, one of them mentioned a man named Ed."

"I can't believe Eduardo betrayed me. I thought he was my friend." Bryan placed his hand on Jan's arm. "I made a mess, didn't I?"

She clasped his hand. When did pencil-pushing Bryan get calluses and scrapes? "You said you work for Amanda's father. What kind of work?"

Bryan cleared his throat. "Construction."

"Really?"

"Yeah. I'm not using my own social security number or real name so the likes of Harold and Tom can't locate me."

"What's changed now?"

"Amanda and I want to get married. I need to clear up this business so I don't have to hide anymore." He fingered his beard. "Last month, I sent the flash drive containing the evidence I collected to the Insurance Commission. They probably opened an investigation about the time Harold and Tom began harassing you."

Jan nodded. "Are those their real names?"

"Yeah. They're brothers."

"They told me."

Mockingbirds squawked in the overhead branches.

"Jan, are we okay?"

She stared at the man who'd caused her so many sleepless nights. His story had filled in the gaps and had given her one very important piece of information. He no longer had any hold on her heart. She was free. "Yes, Bryan. We're okay." She smiled at him. "But please, for all our sakes, call your mother. She needs to hear your voice."

"I will as soon as this insurance business is cleared up. I don't want to put her in danger, too."

"Can I at least tell her I've seen you?"

"No, not yet. I'll visit her soon. Be wary of Tom and Harold.

"I will." Jan stood and when Hatch rose, gave him his jacket. "By the way, this is KC, my…boyfriend."

Bryan stood, too. "Jan, I'm sorry."

She held up her hand. "Don't say anymore. Get your name cleared, call your mother, and…and I hope you and Amanda—"

A shot rang out.

CHAPTER 39

Inherent instinct kicked in. Hatch grabbed Jan and pulled her to the ground. "Get down, everyone." He glanced at the other bench. Amanda knelt on the gravel beside a prone Bryan. Was he wounded?

In the background, a motorbike engine roared. The shot came from the same direction as the sound. Hatch glanced toward the raw brush behind the bank. The engine noise diminished in seconds. He prayed the shooter was on the bike and crawled over to Bryan. Amanda had pulled aside his jacket and blood oozed over his right shoulder.

People poured out of the bank. "Call an ambulance. And the cops. Tell them the shooter escaped on a motorbike," Hatch yelled.

He glanced at Bryan's face. His eyes were closed and his mouth gaped. He was unconscious. Hatch felt for a pulse. None.

Jan had inched closer.

He began chest compressions and said to her, "I

noticed an AED on the wall in the teller's area. Get it, please. And a first aid kit."

She pushed her way through the crowd.

"What's an AED?" Amanda's voice quivered. "Why are you doing that? Has his heart stopped?"

"Yes. Maybe the shock of getting shot. Jan's getting an Automated External Defibrillator. To…shock his heart. When I remove my hands, quickly unbutton his shirt." He was aware more blood oozed from the wound with each compression but Hatch couldn't stop. Bryan still had no pulse.

"Here, Hatch." Jan had already unzipped the labeled canvas bag and placed it beside Bryan. "What else can I do?"

"Take the gauze out of the kit, please, then keep clear." Hatch turned on the machine, removed the pads, and placed them on Bryan's chest. When the animated voice advised the user to administer a shock, he said, "Stay back, everyone." He pushed the button, Bryan's shoulders rose a fraction in response, and seconds later, the voice instructed him to administer chest compressions.

Hatch had to shock Bryan a second time before his heart beat again. Breathing hard, he sat on the gravel then took the gauze from Jan and wadded it up over Bryan's wound. "Amanda, keep pressure here."

"Okay." She pressed on the gauze and Bryan winced.

Hatch removed the disposable pads and closed the

bag.

Bryan opened his eyes, blinked, and searched the faces staring at him. He focused on Amanda. "Hi, darling. What happened?"

She pulled his shirt over his exposed chest. "You've been shot. But the ambulance is on its way." Jutting her chin toward Hatch, she said, "Thank you for saving his life."

He nodded, stood, and helped Jan to her feet. The EMTs would pick up where he left off. "Do you want to go inside or wait out here?"

The wail of sirens drew closer.

"I'll stay here." Jan slipped her hand into his.

If it wasn't winter, he might have melted.

Minutes later, Bryan lay on a gurney, attended by two EMT's. Amanda hovered close by, concern adding a few wrinkles to her forehead.

When the police arrived, they took statements, and when they questioned Jan, she gave them Sergeant Voss's contact information.

Walking with her to her vehicle, Hatch placed his arm around her shoulders. "Are you okay?"

"Yes. According to the EMT, Bryan's wound isn't life-threatening. You assured me Margaret is only a friend, and I'm free."

"Free?" He figured he knew what she meant but he wanted her to acknowledge the truth.

"Bryan didn't leave because I failed as a fiancée, and he has no claim to my heart."

He squeezed her shoulder. "That's music to my ears."

CHAPTER 40

Thunder and lightning greeted Jan when she awoke the next morning. She snuggled under the covers and recalled the previous day's events. Hatch confirmed Margaret's place in his life. Bryan explained why he left. Bryan shot.

She rubbed her eyes Yeah. It all happened. Time to move on. Such a glib expression if a person is stuck in the past. She had been, but now she was free. After shooing Moxie off the bed, Jan threw back the covers and waltzed around the room. She was free from Bryan and felt confident and—dare she say—happy.

What should she do on her first day of freedom? Visit Delaney and her bloodhounds again? Paint? Or…

Jan's phone rang. She unplugged it and checked the screen. Sergeant Voss. They'd located the abandoned motorbike, but no sign of Harold or Tom. Jan pursed her lips and ran down the stairs to feed Moxie and make coffee. Lots of coffee.

While she sipped the brew, her phone rang again. Unknown caller. For a second, she froze. But it couldn't be another harassing call. Bryan had exposed the fraud. She answered and was surprised to hear Amanda's voice.

"Bryan is going to be all right. The bullet went straight through muscle and he should be discharged tomorrow. He's out of surgery and is still sleeping."

"That's good news. How long will you stay in San Antonio?"

"We're not sure. Bryan called his mother yesterday and it took a while to convince her he was in town. He said she sounded…strange. Not quite herself."

"I've noticed the same thing. It might be her medication." What else could she say?

"Marybeth also said she doesn't drive anymore so she can't visit Bryan, but she did invite us to stay with her."

"That's a good idea." At least it would be for Marybeth.

"Bryan wants to know if you have any insight into Marybeth's situation."

Jan had so much to share but needed to speak to Bryan face-to-face. "I'll talk to him when he gets home."

"Okay. I hope there's nothing seriously wrong with her."

"Bryan needs to check on her medication. I'm sure that's the problem. Thanks for calling, and let me know if I can do anything for you." Jan made another cup of coffee. Should she check on Marybeth? Not driving was a new concern.

She decided to leave Marybeth's issues for Bryan and Amanda to sort out. They'd be there tomorrow. She carried her mug upstairs but her phone rang again before she could turn on the shower. Teagan. Voss had contacted her and she knew all about the shooting.

"Did Bryan explain his actions?"

"He did." Jan gave her an abbreviated version of his account. "Now I know why those two goons targeted me."

"And Voss suspects one of them shot Bryan."

"So do I." They chatted a few minutes longer, and then Teagan had to return to her assignment.

Jan stared at her phone. "No more calls, please." She showered and dressed in sweats, prepared for a lazy day. Chores at her leisure or not at all. Order a pizza for lunch.

Her first task was to unload all the painting supplies she'd brought home from the gallery studio. She'd tossed Richard's portrait, but sorting the paint tubes in the cabinet reminded her of his duplicity. "How could I have been so gullible?" Arranging the brushes by type, she rolled her eyes. He had been very persuasive.

Since she was in her studio, she tidied up the place, counted the blank canvases, checked which paint colors needed replenishment, and then made a list. Feeling peckish, she ordered a supreme pizza and ran downstairs anxious for the delivery. She loaded the dishwasher and wiped the counters and the table. While filling Moxie's water bowl, the doorbell ring startled her.

"Great. Early delivery." Halfway to the front door, she stopped, returned to the kitchen, and hunted for her phone. The camera did not show a pizza delivery, but Hatch.

She opened the door, tongue-tied and embarrassed for her sloppy appearance. "Hello."

"I was going to call first, but Sophie has an unexpected playdate with a friend from daycare and I took advantage of the situation."

"I ordered pizza. Can you stay for lunch?"

"Sure, but I'm not hungry."

Jan entered her den and sat on the sofa. Could she be bold and ask outright? Yep. Her newfound confidence stepped in. "Why are you here, Hatch?"

He perched on the edge of an armchair and faced her, elbows on his knees. "First, have you heard from Bryan? How is he?"

"Amanda called. He will be fine and may be discharged tomorrow. Which is good news, however, they are going to stay with Marybeth for a while." She frowned. "Did I tell you she lives two doors down and attends the church I went to? It's been hard with her that close, especially these last few weeks when she accused me of killing Bryan."

"Why would she say that now, a year after he left?"

"I don't know. In my opinion, she hasn't been thinking rationally recently. Having Bryan with her might be a good idea."

"Will it bother you if he's that close?"

She hiked a shoulder. "I'd rather not have him next door, and who knows how long he and Amanda might stay. Marybeth mentioned moving to a retirement home before all this nonsense with Harold and Tom."

"Interesting. Anything from Voss?"

"They found the motorbike, but no trace of the shooter."

He rubbed his chin. "That's a lot on your plate, and I'm going to add to the load. Are you ready? I have so much to say and hope you will indulge me."

"What's on your mind?"

"More like what's on my heart."

Ooh. Heavy. "Go on."

Huffing out a breath, he clasped his hands. "During one of our conversations, you said I needed help and I admitted I am seeing a therapist, Dr. Patrick Rose, a college friend and he knew Laura." Hatch warded off Jan's attempted interruption. "I want to explain. Okay?"

"Of course." His intensity spilled over her and she leaned forward.

"I have to go back in time." He paused. "Laura committed suicide."

Jan gasped but held back her words. A heavy knot formed close to her heart.

"She suffered severe postpartum depression and I

missed the signs. I knew she was tired and frustrated because Sophie had colic. I had no idea of the extent of her depression." He hung his head for a moment.

"Would you like something to drink?"

"Please. A glass of water."

Jan hurried to the kitchen and the doorbell rang. "That's the pizza. I'll be right back." She collected the box which she placed on the kitchen table. It would keep.

"Go ahead and eat. It won't bother me." Hatch glanced at Jan when she returned to the den with his water. He downed it all.

"No. I'll wait. Continue, please." Where was he going with his confession? And why share these intimate moments with her?

"About six months ago, it hit me that I'd failed Laura. That I'd dismissed her need. I became angry with myself for my neglect. The guilt piled on month after month and I couldn't do anything about it, except help other women who might be in a similar situation." He harumphed. "But I went overboard and perceived depression where there wasn't any, or interpreted signs of mild depression as something far worse. I couldn't help myself."

"I'm a victim of your obsession."

"Yes. You summarized my problem very succinctly." He straightened in the chair and leaned back. "So, I'm here to apologize again."

"What happened six months ago?"

"Aha. That is exactly what Patrick asked. Sophie said she's the only kid who is always picked up by her dad at daycare and wanted to know why she didn't have a mother."

"Poor child." Jan almost choked on the words. No wonder Hatch's behavior changed at that time.

"My explanation to Sophie brought on my anger. Not toward God, but myself. I had deprived my daughter of her mother."

"That's harsh."

"But the truth. If I'd been aware of her state of mind, I could have, would have intervened." He set his empty glass on the coffee table, walked to the large window, and then turned. "In my latest session with Patrick, he quoted Eckhart Tolle's profound statement. 'Where there is anger, there is always pain underneath'. That alone, helped me tame my anger. I realized it came from my pain. Above all, I had allowed my personal battles to impact my relationship with God. I was ashamed when I read my business card. 'Specializing in Christian-based principles'. Ha. Not for a long time."

"Why are you telling me this? I don't think I can help you." Not when she was trying to restore her crumbled relationship with God.

"I will continue to see Patrick until we both agree I've accepted what happened and the role I played." He walked to the sofa and sat beside Jan. "I hope I convinced you yesterday that you are special to me. Do you want to know how you can help?"

She nodded.

"Think about my question before you answer, please. Do you want to pursue a relationship with me?"

Crossing her legs, she focused on her purple and gray sneakers. Did she? It didn't take long to decide. "Yes."

"Woohoo." Hatch grinned and placed a hand over his heart. "I'm not finished yet. I had to share what was weighing me down before I could ask you to believe in me. I didn't want to hide anything from you. Based on my experience, a strong human relationship can thrive when built on a solid foundation in Christ."

"I agree that's important."

"When you first came to Deer Park, you said you were looking for a new church home. Does that mean you were unsatisfied with the previous place where you worshipped?"

"Yes. But not because they were teaching against Scripture, although in my opinion, many sermons were shallow and pleasing to the ears. I left because of how I felt."

"Tell me more. I want to understand."

"I'd lost my enthusiasm, partly because I allowed my busy life to take precedence and I felt as if I was going through the motions during the services. I'd become apathetic. I know we gather to worship God, to praise Him. Worship should not be designed to please us, yet we need—"

"We need to participate with open hearts and

minds, conscious of what we are doing and why."

"Exactly." She smiled at him. "God doesn't want to be worshipped by unthinking robots."

Hatch held Jan's hand. "Bear with me while I put on my counselor hat. The first step to solving a problem is recognizing there is one. Second, admit it to someone. And third, devise a plan."

Jan turned on the seat and faced him. "Okay, then part of my plan will be to get back to the basics, to change my attitude. I grew up in the church. I studied the Bible and know it's our guidebook."

"I also grew up in a church-going family. I can quote chapter and verse on many subjects, but it doesn't matter how knowledgeable we are about the scriptures, sometimes it takes another person to point out the obvious. Patrick reminded me of Hebrews 10:22. I've memorized the scripture. 'Let us draw near to God with a sincere heart in full assurance of faith, having our hearts sprinkled to cleanse us from a guilty conscience.' Part of my plan is to forgive myself. We can't go back and fix our mistakes, but we can learn from them." Hatch inhaled deeply. "We *must* learn from them, but we do not need to let shame and guilt control us when we have the assurance that if we confess our sins, God will forgive us. Principles found in I John 1:9."

Jan hadn't heard anything new from Hatch, but his words hurled several barbs into her soul. They were reminders of the truths she knew but had buried in the dark recesses of her soul. "I need to apply those lessons to my life, too."

He scooted closer. "There's one more phase in my plan. Whenever I encounter a woman whom I think is depressed, I'll remember what you said about being a victim of my obsession. Unless of course, she's a client and admits to being depressed."

Jan laughed out loud and then hushed. Hatch was sitting awfully close.

He ran a thumb across her cheek.

The caress opened her heart to Mr. Right.

The fingers of his other hand trailed up her arm to her shoulder, then her cheek, finally nestling in her hair. He brought her closer, his lips hovering over hers, hesitating as if to give her time to pull away. Her breath mingled with his, all thoughts of anything but this moment swept from her mind as his lips covered hers. The gentle kiss, promising passion to come, chased all memories of Bryan, Harold, Tom, and Richard to Pluto. She reached her arms around his neck and felt safe, secure, and special in his embrace. When they pulled apart they stared into each other's eyes and would have repeated the kiss if his phone hadn't rung.

"Rats." He pulled it from his pocket and checked the screen. "It's the mother of Sophie's friend. Hi, Nicole." He listened a moment. "Okay, I'll be right there." Returning his phone to his pocket, he said, "The playdate is over. I guess I'll see you tomorrow?"

Jan snuggled against him. "I don't want this day to end. How about I order more pizza and you come over for supper?"

"Sounds good, but I have a couple of errands to run, and then I'll pick up the pizza and be back here about six."

"That'll give me time to complete my chores and change."

He tweaked her cheek. "I know you mean your clothes, but don't change. If you were any more perfect, I'd have to build you a pedestal."

Easing off the sofa, Jan covered her hot cheeks with her hands. "I could get used to this attention, but, please, quit with the perfection label."

He chuckled, picked up his jacket, and headed to the front door. "There's something we can do to strengthen our bond. We—"

"We can pray together."

"Great minds…" He opened his arms. "Come here, my dear."

Nestled against his chest, she bowed her head.

Hatch's head rested on hers. "It's been a while since I prayed from my heart. Bear with me, please." He cleared his throat. "Father, God, thank you for the avenue of prayer. We come before you as children who seek your guidance. Speak to us through Your Word. Thank you for bringing Jan into my life." His voice cracked.

Touched by his display of emotion, Jan added, "And, Father, please bless this new journey we're embarking upon. In Jesus's name. Amen."

"Amen."

Silence for a few seconds.

He opened the door. "See you soon."

After he left, Jan leaned against the door, heart close to bursting.

CHAPTER 41

Delicious aromas of vanilla and peaches swirled around the kitchen. The only thing Jan could make that turned out perfect every time was an easy peach cobbler, a recipe from Mother's friend, Neva. Simple ingredients Jan had on hand most of the time. Flour, milk, and sugar. Butter, baking powder, vanilla, and of course a can of fruit. Mix all together and pop it in the oven. Done.

She'd made a salad to accompany the pizza and placed the bowl on the kitchen table, along with plates, napkins, and silverware, to create a more casual atmosphere to match her denim overalls and pink checked shirt.

The doorbell rang and her phone showed her guests on the porch. She opened the door, and a bout of shyness overcame her. She lowered her head and clasped her hands.

"Hello, again." Hatch ushered Sophie inside while carrying two pizza boxes.

Jan closed the door, not sure what to do next.

She needn't have worried. He lowered his head and kissed her. "I told Sophie that we like each other very much."

Jan touched Sophie's cheek. "And I like you very much, too."

The child blushed and removed her jacket. "Here, Daddy."

Hatch hung their jackets on the rack by the door.

Clasping Jan's hand, Sophie skipped down the hall. "Daddy says I can't call you Paint Lady anymore. My teachers at school are Miss Gloria and Miss Angie. Can I call you Miss Jan?" They reached the kitchen and Sophie looked up at Jan, head tilted and smiling.

"I think Miss Jan is perfect."

Hatch had set the boxes on the counter and winked at her. "See. Miss Perfect."

"Hush."

"Where's Moxie?" Sophie looked under the table and wandered into the pantry.

"She's probably upstairs on my bed, but she'll come down now that she hears my company."

As if she'd been waiting for her cue, the cat sauntered into the kitchen and headed for the child.

"I think she likes me." Sophie picked up Moxie and kissed her head.

"Jan, do you mind if we don't eat right away?" Hatch ran his hand through his hair, mussing up the waves.

"Of course not."

"Sophie, remember what we talked about? Please go sit in the den."

"Can Moxie come too?"

"Sure."

Sophie left the kitchen, telling the cat all about her playdate.

"What's going on, Mr. Hatcher?"

"I did a lot of thinking this afternoon and I have a solution to one of your problems." He paused. "Sell your house and move, and you'll never have to see Marybeth or Bryan Buchanan again."

"But I don't want to move. I love this place and there's my studio."

"Then how about we buy another house with a studio, lots of bedrooms, a large yard…"

Jan looked at Hatch, trying to decipher his exact meaning. "Another house?"

"Yes. If I sell my house and you sell your house, we'll have to live somewhere!"

"Hatch?"

He knelt in front of her. Taking her hand in both of his, he gazed at her. "Janyth, do you love me?"

She swallowed, then whispered, "Yes, Hatch, I love you."

"Good, because I love you. Will you buy a house with me? Will you be a mother to Sophie and any other children we may be blessed with? Will you marry me?" He pulled a small jewelry box from his pocket and opened it. It contained a purple and pink plastic gimmick ring.

Stupefied, she knelt too. "I will."

"This monstrosity is a placeholder. I want us to choose rings together." He wrapped his arms around her, drawing her to him, his lips closing over hers in a kiss full of promise and longing.

Jan could have remained in his arms forever, but a voice from the den interrupted the moment.

"Daddy, I'm hungry. Can I come in now?"

They pulled apart and Jan giggled. "Come, Sophie. Supper's ready."

The pizza was a hit, as expected, and so was the cobbler. "I'll clean up later."

They sat together on the sofa and watched Sophie play with Moxie but the cat had had enough and ran off. Sophie crawled up into Hatch's lap. "Do you have any books for kids, Miss Jan?"

"Hmm. Let me think. Yes, I have a few I kept from my childhood. They're in the garage. I'll be right back." She rummaged through one of the tubs and found a couple of books.

As soon as she returned to the den, Sophie asked, "Miss Jan, can you read me a story?"

"Please," prompted Hatch.

"Pleeese."

"I'd love to." She held the book so all three could see the pictures. *The Wide-Mouthed Frog* kept them smiling, but by the time Jan finished *Giggle, Giggle, Quack,* Sophie's eyes drooped and her head rested on

Hatch's shoulder. Jan quietly placed the book on the coffee table and stood.

"She's had a busy day." Hatch covered Sophie with the small throw rug at one end of the sofa, and he and Jan settled on the other end.

"I wonder where Harold and Tom are? Hope they took a slow boat to—"

The doorbell rang.

Jan jumped up to answer it before the chimes woke Sophie, but the noise continued. Soon, pounding and yelling accompanied the chimes. She'd left her phone in the kitchen, but as soon as she checked the peephole, she opened the door.

Marybeth stood on the porch, blood gushing from her forehead. She staggered and collapsed across the threshold. "Help," she whispered.

Hatch, who had followed Jan to the door, said, "Can you stand? Hold onto my arm."

Marybeth stood by grabbing onto Hatch.

"Come, sit down, Marybeth." Jan guided her to an armchair in the front room. "I'll get some towels."

She ran to the kitchen, yanked a roll of paper towels off the counter, and grabbed her phone. On the way past the den, she glanced at the sofa. Sophie slept peacefully.

"Here, Hatch." She handed him the roll and then called for an ambulance.

He took a wad of paper and placed it on her temple. "The wound doesn't look very deep, but something else is going on here. I can't get a word out of her. She'd almost catatonic, and—"

"I thought I'd find Marybeth here."

Hatch and Jan turned at the sound of Inez Nash's voice.

"How did you get in?" Jan slipped her phone into her pocket.

"You shouldn't have left the door open." Mrs. Nash took a couple of steps into the room.

"I forgot I had."

Hatch continued to hold the paper to Marybeth's head. "What do you want? Are you responsible for this?" He nodded toward the victim.

"You could say that. Me and my…sons." Inez grinned, the door slammed, and two men joined her. Harold and Tom.

Cogwheels turned lickety-split in Jan's brain. Connections began to make a modicum of sense. Inez only appeared on the scene a few weeks before her sons harassed Jan.

Hatch grabbed Marybeth's hand. "You must hold this to your head, Marybeth. Do you hear me?" He released the padding. The injured woman kept her hand on the paper and he placed himself between Jan and the uninvited guests.

"What did you do to her?" Hatch pointed to Marybeth.

Inez chuckled. "Nothing, other than make her take her medication. She did the rest on her own."

"Medication. But you told me—" Jan shifted her gaze from Inez to the pathetic figure of Marybeth, slouched in the chair. "Did you mess with her pills? I didn't notice changes in her behavior until you moved in and befriended her."

Inez looped her arm through Tom's. "Something like that. We needed information about Bryan."

"But she didn't know anything. Neither did I." Jan shook her head, remembering all the weird incidents that happened to her. "Whose idea was it to dig up my tree?"

Harold raised his hand. "That would be me. I had the old woman convinced you'd buried Bryan under it. But Tom did his share of stuff."

"Yeah. I slashed your tire." He chuckled. "That was fun."

Hatch folded his arms. "You must have given Marybeth some powerful drugs."

"Some psychotropic something or other," Inez said.

"She looks in bad shape, and you still haven't told us why you're here." Jan gave Marybeth another wad of clean towels and tossed the blood-soaked wad.

The three villains looked at each other, the mother in the middle of her tall sons.

"Okay, I'll tell them." Inez stepped to the sofa and sat down.

Harold and Tom remained in the entryway, and Jan and Hatch hovered over Marybeth.

"Our old lady here was supposed to take a fatal dose of pills tonight. But some detective visited her earlier to tell her Bryan will be discharged tomorrow."

"How do you know about that?" Jan asked.

Inez held up her hand. "One story at a time. Marybeth wouldn't swallow all the pills, so we had a little shoving match. She fell and hit her head. She's fast on her feet, and before I knew it, she'd made her way to your door."

"Now that you've brought all of this to my house, what's next?"

Harold reached into his pockets and pulled out four pill bottles, two in each hand. "Y'all are going to join Mrs. Buchanan on her psychedelic trip."

Jan leaned closer to Hatch and gripped his arm.

He turned to her and whispered, "Don't worry. I hear sirens."

She nodded once and looked at the men in front of her. Suddenly, all of the misery they'd inflicted on her over the past months, broiled over and erupted in red-hot lava. She pushed away from Hatch. "And what if I don't want to swallow any of your nasty pills? What if I kick and scream?" She took a step closer to Harold. "It's too late for you anyway. The insurance company is under investigation. The cops are looking for you."

Inez struggled to stand. "Who do you think is going to stop us? Bryan tried and look what happened to him."

"Bryan. Did you say, Bryan?" Marybeth stirred.

"Bryan. Don't hurt my Bryan." The bulky woman leaped from the chair and landed full on Inez, knocking her to the floor.

Hatch took advantage of the distraction. He flashed past Jan, arms and legs flying in all directions, and Tom lay groaning, clutching his jaw.

"What in the world?"

Hatch grinned at Jan and flexed his biceps. "Didn't I tell you I played college football? Haven't forgotten how to tackle. Now for Harold."

But he threw the pill bottles at Hatch and charged at Jan.

With his enormous hands around her throat, he said. "Don't try anything. One hard squeeze and she's gone."

What was it with men and her throat? Jan thrashed about, more out of anger than fear.

Hatch held up both hands. "Okay, okay. Don't hurt her. You can get out of here, Harold. Listen." He pointed to the door. "Those sirens are coming this way. The cops will be here any minute. Let Jan go and you can leave out the back door. Go."

Harold hesitated, relaxing his hold a tad. Jan scratched at his fingers and kept her gaze glued to Hatch's face. Blood pounded in her head like claps of thunder. Pain encircled her neck and she struggled for air.

"Come on, Harold. Let her go and get out of here." Hatch stood, feet apart, arms by his sides.

Jan grabbed one of Harold's fingers and bent it backward as far as possible.

He groaned and released her. She staggered away from him, choking for air.

As Harold ran past Hatch, he struck out his leg. Harold fell, sprawling face-first in the hall. Hatch pounced on him, grabbing his wrists and kneeing him in the back.

"Jan, sweetheart, are you all right?"

She nodded.

"Good. Can you get the door?"

Sirens wailed outside. Jan opened the door and emergency personnel and police officers rushed in.

EPILOGUE

Eyes closed, Jan waited beside Hatch's Jeep.

"Okay, you can open your eyes now." Sophie giggled. "Come on, Miss Jan."

Jan blinked. In front of her was the house they'd frequently viewed online. A two-story, colonial-style, surrounded by manicured lawns, shrubs, and flower beds, all thriving in the spring weather. "Online pictures don't do it justice. The house is so beautiful, sweetheart. Large and beautiful."

"The realtor showed me around yesterday. Lots of bedrooms and one looks like it'll make a great studio. Big windows and room for counters and a sink."

"I gather it's back on the market now?"

"Yes. The sale fell through. Our realtor will be here in about fifteen minutes."

Hatch slipped his arm around her shoulders. "We can peek through the windows while we wait."

"I'm so thankful it's available. I fell in love with it online. Isn't that silly?"

"Not at all. I understand why. If we purchase it

now, you can arrange for a room to be renovated for your studio. The work could be done by the end of next month, just in time for the wedding."

Sophie had run up the sidewalk and now skipped back to them. "There's a surprise in the backyard."

"Hush, young lady. Don't expose our little secret."

"Okay, enough subterfuge. What surprise?"

Hatch led Jan around the house and opened the gate to the spacious backyard. Close to the fence stood a huge oak tree. From one of the branches, a rope swing swayed in the breeze.

Jan stopped walking and covered her gaping mouth with her hands. She turned to Hatch, her heart brimming over with love. "It's perfect, my darling."

THE END

Neva's Peach Cobbler

1 cup flour   1 cup sugar   1 cup milk

2 tsp baking powder   ¼ cup butter
medium can of fruit, drained   pinch of salt

Grease a 9 x 9 baking dish with the butter. Mix milk, sugar, flour, baking powder, and salt. Pour into dish. Add the fruit and give the mixture a quick stir. Bake at 350° for 1 hour. Serve hot with cream or ice cream.

Dear Reader:

I hope you enjoyed Jan's story. The incident where she tells Hatch her full name happened to my college roommate whose name was Janyth.

How do you think her early diagnosis of scoliosis affected her adult life? I spoke with several women who experienced many back surgeries and they all said their teenage years were the worst.

I'm excited to continue with Delaney's story, and then Teagan's story. Jan's sisters are intriguing characters, too.

If you liked this story, please consider leaving a review. Reviews are important to authors.

Sincerely,

Valerie Massey Goree

BIO:
Award winner Valerie Massey Goree resides in the beautiful Hill Country, northwest of San Antonio.

After serving as missionaries in her home country of Zimbabwe and raising two children, Valerie and her husband, Glenn, a native Texan, moved to Texas. She worked in the public school system for many years, focusing on students with special needs. Now retired, Valerie spends her time writing, traveling, and spoiling her grandchildren.

Valerie loves to hear from her readers.

Connect with Valerie:

- Check her website to learn more about her romantic suspense novels and Glenn's non-fiction books: valeriegoreeauthor.com

- You can sign up for her quarterly newsletter and email her from the website.

- Facebook Author Page. Valerie Goree, Author
https://www.facebook.com/profile.php?id=6156177591 6508

- GoodReads and BookBub

Other Books By Valerie Massey Goree,
(All are described on her website.)

Texas Suspense:
Deceive Me Once
Colors of Deceit

Stolen Lives Trilogy:
Weep in the Night
Day of Reckoning
Justice at Dawn

Stand Alone:
Forever Under Blue Skies

My Mother's Secret:
Shadows of Time
Every Hidden Thing

From England with Love and…Dissension Trilogy:
Book 1: Meet Me Where the Windrush Flows